MW01277606

Getting Acquainted

Getting Acquainted

JOHN GORDON

Copyright © 2012 by John Gordon.

ISBN: Softcover   978-1-4691-4607-2
             Ebook   978-1-4691-4608-9

All rights reserved. No part of this book may be reproduced or transmitted in any form
or by any means, electronic or mechanical, including photocopying, recording, or by
any information storage and retrieval system, without permission in writing from the
copyright owner.

This is a work of fiction. Names, characters, places and incidents either are the product
of the author's imagination or are used fictitiously, and any resemblance to any actual
persons, living or dead, events, or locales is entirely coincidental.

This book was printed in the United States of America.

To order additional copies of this book, contact:
Xlibris Corporation
1-888-795-4274
www.Xlibris.com
Orders@Xlibris.com
110149

CONTENTS

ERNIE AND CHICO

"What time is it?"

"Not too late. Does it matter?"

"Sure it matters. Time matters."

"No not really. We haven't been here very long. You got here maybe twenty, thirty minutes ago, I guess. Believe me, time really doesn't matter. I mean it's significant, important sometimes too, but it doesn't really matter. What's the rush?"

"There isn't any rush. I just like to know. It's a reference point, a focal point. I like to know what time it is and where I am and where I'm going, stuff like that."

"Fair enough, but we're here now and there's no place to go."

"That's cool, see it isn't so important once I know, you know?"

"I guess. You're kind of funny. I'd forgotten that."

"Anyway, the other day I was thinking about a kid named Ernie Hahn."

"Ernie? Ernie Hahn?"

"Yeah, I grew up with him. Well, he moved away when I was about twelve or thirteen I guess. His dad got transferred to Massachusetts, but we spent a lot of time together until then."

"Did you miss him?"

"No, not really, he was about four years older than me, and he had started high school, and then I got sent to Prep, but we hung out together when we were real little. He had an older brother, too; Chip, or maybe Skip. That's strange, I don't remember. Slip? No, that was Buddy. We used to call Buddy Hiller, Slip. Anyway, Chip or Skip died in Vietnam, but that wasn't what I was thinking about. I was thinking about Ernie.

"We played Little League together. Not really together so much, even though his mother usually drove us down to the field, but like I said, he was older. Our league was pretty good about putting brothers on the same team, so Ernie played for the Lions, just like his older brother, poor dead Chip, or Skip. I didn't have an older brother, both of mine were, are younger, so I was the first Monroe to come along and I got put on the Ukes."

"Ukes?"

"Hey, no laughing, I was very proud to be a Uke. Teams were sometimes named after the sponsors, and our team was sponsored by the Ukrainian Sportsmen's Club. They were a bunch of old eastern European guys that drank shots and beer in a little clubhouse they had down in Scaife. We would go in there after games, coach would take us, and it was weird. None of them spoke English. It was dark and smelled like cabbage. I'm pretty sure they all worked at the steel mill. Other teams were the Lions, like I said, or the Bears, the Cubs, Pirates, Indians. There were the New Car Dealers and Staiano's."

"Right, Staiano's was the appliance store."

"Uh huh, electronics, I think, but we were the Ukes. We had really cool uniforms, like the Dodgers. They were white with blue piping and Ukes written in script across the chest. They looked clean, bright, and real crisp. Other teams had cool clubhouses; the Lions especially. They had a chill place, and they all struck me as richer than us. They were the wealthier kids whose parents drove them to games in fancy cars. My mother had a Ford station wagon that always smelled like sour milk and baby puke. I rode my old Schwinn to the field when we weren't playing the Lions and I didn't get a ride with Ernie's mother. Yeah, I was a Uke, and damn proud of it too. Oh, sorry, excuse me."

"No problem, so what about Ernie?"

"Ernie was the man. I always looked up to him. He was the superstar on his team. We didn't have a superstar. Every other team had the big, strong twelve year-old that pitched, or played center field, and hit home runs. The superstars always batted fourth. That reminds me of that Springsteen song, *Glory Days*. Everybody had a kid that could throw that speedball by you and make you look like a fool; not us. We didn't have that guy. I guess I was the closest thing to a star on the Ukes and I played shortstop and led off."

"Led off?"

"Batted first, when you bat at the top of the order, you lead off. Anyway, once Ernie and I were playing Rescue 8, it was an old TV show."

"Yes, I remember."

"Yeah, and Ernie tied a rope around my waist and he was pulling me up onto his front porch that was built over their garage, and the rope slipped up to my neck. He was strangling me, but I couldn't yell. Besides, I trusted him, and I thought it was part of the plan. I woke up in the Hahn's kitchen with Ernie's mother and sisters standing over me. His oldest sister had seen that he was choking me and had run up and saved me, and poor Ernie got in trouble. I went up to his bedroom, and he was sitting on the floor crying. He got real embarrassed and yelled at me to get out and told me that he hated me, and I thought it was because I got him in trouble. Years later his sister told me that he thought he had killed me, or at least really hurt me, and it scared him so much that he ran up to his room crying. She told me that at a beer party on the fourth of July."

"Anyway."

"Yeah, anyway, I was thinking about Ernie in this one baseball game the Ukes were playing the Lions. He was probably twelve, the star of his team, and I was probably nine or so, maybe even eight. We were up at bat, and Ernie was playing center field when one of our guys smacked a line drive that went all the way to the fence. I was standing in the dugout, we had cool dugouts, and I knew this was gonna be good. I was thinking that Ernie was gonna snatch that ball up and fire a bullet to second base and nail our guy. I don't really know who I was rooting for; us or Ernie. But when he got to the fence—he was fast, real fast—and he got to that fence and reached for the ball, and then his foot slipped. It slid right under the fence, and he couldn't get it out. He was stuck. He had the ball in his hand, and our guy is rounding first, and everyone can see that Ernie's got his foot stuck, and everybody's yelling like crazy, and then the damndest thing . . . oh, sorry."

"Go on."

"Without missing a beat, Ernie flips the ball to the left fielder that's charging up to him and the kid bare hands it and swivels and fires it into the infield."

"Did he get the runner?"

"I don't remember. I don't remember anything else about that game, or really about any other game. I don't know who won, or who lost, or what happened next, but I'll never forget how cool Ernie flipped that ball. He was so calm. It was like they'd practiced it or something. The kid was just so cerebral under fire, know what I mean? No panic, just deal with the situation by flipping the ball to his teammate like he'd done it a hundred times. There was no hesitation, just an instinctive reaction. It was poetic. It was ballet, man. I was totally speechless. It was just so Ernie."

"Just, so Ernie."

"I always wanted to be like him. I wanted to live my life like that: focused, disciplined, seeing the whole picture, know what I mean?"

"Sure."

"I wanted to have that presence of mind, to be aware of everything, every situation, to know what to do, and have the confidence to just do it. I wanted to live my life with teammates like Ernie. I don't know, I guess I've always wanted people to depend on me like I always depended on Ernie. I never had that."

"Yes you did. You've lived a good life. People have depended on you. You've been responsible and considerate. You're one of the most sentient people that I've met in a long time. Maybe you learned that from Ernie."

"We learn from everybody, from all of our experiences, good and bad."

"If we're paying attention."

"Right, I learned from a lot of people. Chico taught me how to work. When I look back on it, I see that he was as obsessive a control freak as I was. But he taught me how to work. He taught me to think ahead, to project, and he was a team player too. Chico was all about doing things efficiently, and making work easy and fun. Heck, he was only a teenager himself. I'll bet he went on to be a big success. Dad tried to hire him after he graduated from college, but Chico had other plans."

"Did you ever see Ernie again?"

"Yep, I saw him at that fourth of July party with his sister a couple of years after they'd moved, and then I saw him at a wedding three or four years after that. He was doing pretty well. He'd moved up to Massachusetts and won the state wrestling championship two years in a row. That didn't surprise any of us."

"Pretty big accomplishment."

"No kidding, but he was a tough kid, like I said. He and his brother were both tough, but more than that, too. They were disciplined. They were dedicated. I think pretty much any kid that comes out of a western Pennsylvania coal and steel town like Scaife is going to do well against New England kids, but Ernie and Chip were special. I'm almost positive his name was Chip. That's terrible, isn't it?"

"You mean that you can't remember his name?"

"The guy died in Vietnam for crying out loud, but I'm pretty sure his name was Chip. I didn't go to his funeral. I think I was already off and running. I missed both of my grandmother's' funerals, too. I had four or five real lost years when I was just thinking about myself, very selfish."

"I know, but all kids are selfish. We grow, we mature, and we learn slowly by making mistakes, being puzzled and confused from time to time. You weren't exactly being a team player, were you?"

"No. No, I wasn't, and it was a waste too, because I loved being part of a team. I liked being part of something, but I acted so aloof and independent, the lone wolf. It was crap, though. I enjoyed being part of a big family. I played soccer with the same group of guys from seventh grade to my senior year. I even organized an independent soccer team in college. I loved being a hippie. It was part of something, a movement, a purpose with wheels. I liked being in the Navy. I was a camaraderie junkie. I liked wrestling, and I liked skiing, but they were somehow different. They were independent. Oh, you're part of a team, but you're really on your own, you dig? I mean, on a team when you lose you lose as a team. On the mat, if you lose, it's just you . . . but when you win, well . . . then it's really just you. It's strange, though; as much as I liked to win, I always felt sorry for the other kid."

"You're sensitive."

"I guess."

"So, tell me more about Ernie. What do you mean when you say he probably did well?"

"Okay, I think I know where you're going with this. I meant financially, you knew that. I think he made a bucketful of money. That's not always bad, you know. He went to work for an investment firm in Philadelphia, he worked hard, and he made money. That's all I was trying to say, and I don't think that's necessarily bad. Is that important? I don't know. It's a loaded question. Like I said, I didn't much know him after about fourteen years old. I don't know what kind of father he was, or what kind of husband he was, or what kind of neighbor he ended up being. I don't know anything about his politics or his spiritual life, but I know he was a nice kid. He was good, and he was my friend. He grew up in a big family like a lot of us. He was kind and considerate, but he was tough too. He cried when he thought that he had hurt me."

"He could be gentle."

"Yeah, he could be gentle, sure."

"He's a lot like you."

"I always wanted to be a lot like him."

"Yeah, you said that. Sensitive."

"Who?"

"Both of you."

"People change, though."

"Sure, people change. You changed."

"It only takes a moment, a moment in the light. It isn't always a flash of light, not always some kind of lightning bolt spiritual awakening. It's more like just finding yourself in the presence."

"And you find yourself in some sort of presence?"

"Yes, I do. I was real confused about the spiritual stuff early in life, but that's all settled down for me now. I'm real comfortable with the connection I have today. It's all so confusing when you're young. Anxiety is tough, but hey, it's tough for everybody. I never thought the searching would stop, never thought I'd just quit looking for whatever it was I was looking for. I have, though. It wasn't in alcohol or drugs, Carlos Castaneda didn't have it, or any of the early philosophers I read. I tried the eastern religions and Epictetus, Aristotle, Socrates, Plato, the whole dream team. Sometimes the harder you look the harder it is to see. Maybe it was C.S. Lewis. I don't know, but I finally sat down and let it all just catch up to me. It was always there, of course, just following along close enough behind waiting for me to settle down enough to let it in. Some people are lucky enough to get that lightning bolt, but my spiritual awakening was more like a creeping, gathering fog. First it engulfed me, and then there was this sense of clarity like a morning dawn after a night-long thunderstorm: clean and crisp, and so bright it hurt my eyes. I'm definitely living in God's presence, and I'm not shy about it anymore."

"You did a lot of searching."

"Boy, you got that right. I spent a lot of time searching for a power that I could trust and rely on. In some ways, I just wanted a big teddy bear to hold, to tell all my secrets to, to share my fears, anxieties, and triumphs with. I've got that today, but you're right, I had to look under every rock to find it."

13

"How'd that happen?"

"What, finding my higher power? Finding God? Finding you? Oops, that's a little presumptuous, huh? But, okay, it was easy. I just quit looking, like I said. I really hope that I've been able to pass some of that along. You can't live with it all: the turmoil, the stress and clamor, the noise and fear, yeah, the fear. Fear in our culture can be so overwhelming. That all finally went away for me, and I'm hoping that maybe I made it a little easier for some others, too."

"I think you did."

"Thanks, that's nice to hear from you. So the plan for finding is to just quit looking. It's official."

"Okay, that works for me. Didn't you leave something out about Ernie?"

"Like what?"

"Like the compliment."

"Yeah, I did."

"Don't mistake humility for false pride. They're two different sides of the same coin."

"I know. I just . . . well, yeah, it was at that July fourth gig. Ernie said I was the best athlete he'd ever known, and it really threw me. I think you know what I mean. I didn't expect to hear that from him, and I'm not sure I deserved it. He'd been drinking; maybe it was the beer talking. He was the best athlete, clearly."

"He admired you."

"I guess you're right, but I'm not sure how that got turned around. I'd always admired him so much."

"Like you said, people change. You don't know what happened to him when he moved away."

"And you do?"

"Sure. Tell me about Chico."

"Are we done with Ernie?"

"For now. You admired Chico a lot too, right? Was he another rock you had to turn over?"

"Yeah, in some ways he was. Chico was the big brother figure. It's funny how relationships change—develop is a better word, I think. He and I had a weird thing for a long time. Our rolls changed, merged, switched. It was always like a never-ending production with Chico. Our families couldn't have been more different, but we were so alike too. His folks were Buckeyes."

"Huh?"

"Yeah, Ohio State Buckeyes. Chico's father played in the marching band. His big claim to fame was dotting the I during the halftime show against Notre Dame. He was a World War Two naval commander; served on a Destroyer in the Pacific. We were Army. My dad was with the 24th Infantry Division in the Eighth Army serving under General Walker in Korea. He was there the day Walker died in a Jeep accident and Ridgway took command. Chico's dad and my dad watched the Army/Navy game together every year when I was growing up. They were a Crest family, and we used Colgate. They drove GMs and we drove Fords. They used whole milk and real butter, and we used skim milk and margarine. They ate Oreos, and we settled for Hydrox. They liked Coke, and we drank Pepsi. Everything was different, and everything was so much alike."

"That's interesting. How else were they different?"

"I'd rather remember how much we were alike. The whole neighborhood was basically the same. Everybody knew everybody else, and most folks thought they knew everybody else's business. All the families were big—six or eight kids. We all either went to the big Presbyterian Church or to the big Catholic Church down in Scaife. Our dads all worked for the steel mills or the coal mines. I went to the same elementary school that my grandfather went to, and I'm sure Chico's brothers and sisters did too. Like I said, things were different, and things were the same."

"But you felt different."

"Always. From the very beginning I felt different. I felt superior. I'm not ashamed to admit it now. I had a big ego. I was very self-centered, but careful not to show it. I thought I was smarter, but I got terrible grades. I had that street smart thing going, though. I never succumbed to any peer pressure. I was the peer. I was the leader, and my friends looked up to me and followed."

"Grandiose."

"Big time grandiose, but not so obvious about it. I was all about self-deprecation. Self deception is probably more like it. I guess I worked a little bit of the self-pity angle there too. I had the thing with the old man that I played, too."

"What thing with the old man?"

"I'll never forget sitting on Chico's front porch one night with his father and a couple of his younger brothers. We used to stay up late and watch the tube on their porch in the summer. The bugs would be banging off the television screen, and we'd be watching Jackie Gleason or Dean Martin. Chico's dad drank whiskey sours, and we would take turns refilling his glass and taking a little swig of whiskey and then try to hide the smell with a cherry.

"Anyway, one night his dad got going about my dad's girlfriend and it embarrassed the heck out of me. Everybody in the neighborhood knew my dad was running around, but until that night I thought it was a family secret, a real ugly, festering family secret. That stung. As I matured I began to acquire a little humility. I became less egocentric, and I started to realize that I didn't have all the answers. A couple of hard knocks can do that. I had my share of reality checks along the way. I started to become a little less judgmental, a little less smug, and maybe not quite as self-righteous. I started to understand that some of the people that I had felt better than actually had some things to share that I could learn from. It was still pure selfishness, still wanting something someone else had, but it was a crack in the door, you know?"

"I think I do."

"I quit clenching my fists. That was something you learned to do early on in my neighborhood, but I started loosening my grip and letting others in a little bit. Once I got that first chink in my armor and started to realize that I wasn't as important as I thought I was, well, things started slowly getting a little bit better. I began to see that I could learn from some of the unique experiences of others. I had a lot to share myself by that stage in my life, and sharing seemed important. I could tell that it helped. I started to develop a sense of fellowship that included a wider variety of people than teammates, bartenders, other sailors, and one night stands. My motivation changed. My relationships with women started changing too. I had always admired their social instincts and their intuition. Suddenly I realized that I had a real feminine side, and I was cool enough to be okay with it. I genuinely liked females."

"Chico taught you this?"

"Hell, no—oops, sorry. No, Chico was all about masculine lessons. These revelations came after Chico, much later. He was in my life during my anxious years, the years that I was seeking and searching. Those were my years of tension, trying to find my way, my spirit, myself. He helped, 'cause, like we were saying, all that experience was important. It all led to where I am now . . . wherever that is."

"What did you find?"

"Me. Eventually I found me, but the journey was more than just discovering me, it was about finding a way to live with me, and with you too, of course."

"Of course, so getting back to Chico, how did he help?"

"From a practical standpoint, he taught me the basics of how to live, a lot of stuff that I probably should have learned from my father. I mean how to live as a teenage boy in America in the sixties and seventies: how to change a tire, adjust a carburetor, smoke a cigarette, carry a tune, handle a pipe wrench, work, drink beer, flirt, that kind of thing. We used to sing in the park until dawn. Just four or five guys—I was always the youngest—harmonizing Motown tunes and passing around a joint. Well, a lot of stuff my dad probably wouldn't have taught me anyway."

"Probably not."

"Chico gave me my first condom."

"Pretty daring stuff."

"Hey, no sarcasm; I think I carried that thing around in my wallet for five years."

"You're precious."

"Yeah, you're sweet too, big guy."

"Chico."

"Right, Chico. Chico and anxiety and teenage angst. I thought the anxiety was going to kill me. I was so restless, so out of sorts. I was sure I was missing out on everything in life. They were pretty tumultuous times remember, and I was stuck in little boy Keds in Scaife. I always wanted to be where I wasn't, anywhere else, anywhere but where I was. That's why I was always looking for action. I had an incurable wanderlust: Vietnam War protests in D.C., making the hippie scene in San Fran, hitchhiking to Woodstock and Watkins Glen, following the Dead to Golden Gate, Red Rocks, and Colt Park."

"You went to Woodstock?"

"I got sent home by a Pennsylvania State Trooper who picked me up on the Turnpike. I was fourteen years old, man, but I saw Grace Slick at the Spectrum, and the Allmann Brothers at the Beacon, and the New Riders at Fillmore East. Saw Grace and the Airplane in Golden Gate, too.

"I once thought that all of these adventures were separate, that they were segmented and episodic. I know differently now. It's all one big, long, unbroken tapestry. Clearing lots in New Hampshire with a chainsaw under the gaze of Mount Washington was part of the same movie that included pouring concrete foundations in Albuquerque with Mexican guys. Hanging sheetrock in Florida, lining a grain ship in Cleveland; it was all a part of the same story. It was my story. It is my story.

"But the rewards were never enough. It was never about the money or the paycheck or the girl. It was the experience. It was about the journey, not the payoff. It's the moments of our lives that we remember. That's what counts, that's what matters. To a certain degree it's about persistence and focus. That's what Chico taught me. He taught me how to be persistent, to work efficiently, to stick with it, whether that meant, learning to play the harmonica or shooting a single leg take-down.

"He taught me how to be organized. The obsessive compulsiveness that wore off on me gave me the ammunition to fight off the chaos and disorder that I'd always felt swirling around me. I had always felt like things were spinning out of control. Having a philandering father is a dysfunction that a kid blames himself for, but Chico helped put order into my life. Crazy stuff, but smart, too, like we would be sure to carry a pipe wrench from one side of the plant to the other to pick up the ladder that we would need to go with the bucket of paint that we had already left with the brushes and the tarp. That was the kind of planning ahead we did because we knew we'd need that wrench for the job we were going to do after the painting was done. I don't mean to ramble, but that's what Chico gave me. That was his gift, biting off little pieces at a time, chipping away at things. It's like riding a bicycle up a hill at night. The headlight only reveals a little bit of what's ahead of you, so that's what you focus on. You don't see the big, never-ending hill. You break it down in little portions and concentrate on what's in front of you. Stay in the moment, in the present. Take life one little step at a time and before you know it, you're at the top of the hill, the boxcar is unloaded, you've swum through the finish line, and the wall is painted. That's what Chico taught me."

"Wow, good lessons."

"Sure, but, of course he didn't think he was teaching anybody anything. He was just being Chico. He was a man of action, a kid really, but for all the enthusiasm he instilled, it wasn't until much later that I learned to combine initiative with humility and responsibility with gratitude."

"Okay."

"He taught me how to use my brain. It was efficiency, but it was more practicality, always thinking ahead. We never went from one place on a job to another empty handed. We always considered what we might need later, so we saved time and motion, and you know, energy. It was about forward thinking, being intentional, and progressive. We excelled at using our minds, and that training really paid off for me in future jobs, and in running my own business, and of course, in the Navy.

"It saved my life a bunch of times when I was operating behind enemy lines, plotting, strategizing, and trying to stay ahead of the bad guys. It all boils down to strategy and preparation. You got to bring your tools. Life is not a straight line. It's more of a spiral, and man, you got to be prepared."

BUCK

"I found Booger in a dumpster."

"Ouch."

"Damn right, ouch, I mean, darn right, ouch. He was in there with three other little puppies. Somebody had just tossed four newborn pups into a garbage bin."

"That's brutal. Who would do that? How old were they?"

"I don't know, some sick person, that's for sure. They were tiny, maybe only ten days old. That's what the vet said. I took them to this vet that Billy knew right down the road from the apartment. They all died except Booger, and he was touch and go for awhile."

"And Billy is . . . ?"

"Billy's Chico's wife, but she wasn't back then. They got married after Sierra and I, so that was five or six years after I found the puppies. I was living on their couch in Coconut Grove. Chico was going to college, and Billy worked at a little boutique out on Key Biscayne. Baby Booger and I stayed with them for about three months until he pooped out our welcome."

"That's nice."

"Well, he did. I got a job working construction and I had to leave him in the apartment, and well, he made a mess."

"What happened?"

"We left."

"Quit the job?"

"Yeah, I bought an old Willys wagon, and Booger and I boogied."

"Why'd you name the poor dog Booger?"

"That didn't last long. Sierra changed his name anyway, but when I found him in the dumpster they were all so sick, their noses were caked with snot. It's gross, I know, but the vet loaded him up with antibiotics, and little Boog pulled through."

"Go on."

"Yeah, okay, sure, so we packed up and left. I was always doing that, wearing out my welcome and splitting like a thief in the night. But now I had a partner, the greatest little dog in the world. We were attached at the hip. Two thieves cruising for the coast. I'd always wanted to see the Pacific, so we cut through the southern half of the country, stopping to pee and take walks, and finally arrived in California."

"That's a long drive."

"Not so bad. I'd saved up enough to buy this cool old truck from a shrimper out in the Everglades. I put as much cheap oil in it as gas, but that was back in the seventies, fuel was nothing compared to what it is now. We ate in diners and slept under the truck and saw a lot of the country, but I was in a hurry to get to the ocean. I'd never seen the Pacific."

"It's beautiful, huh?"

"Amazing, but my first impression wasn't so good, I guess. Looking back, it seems like we were still in Arizona when I saw the lights of L.A. I got to tell you, Los Angeles freaked me out. I don't know what I was expecting, but like so many things in life, it wasn't what I got. It's pretty neat how I bonded with the puppy on that trip, though. I talked to him constantly, and there was no doubt in my mind that he understood everything I said. I didn't know then that we'd never be really alone again. I didn't know then that he'd get so big either. Those were the last days that he was Booger, and the last nights that he was all mine."

"What happened?"

"What always happens; I met a girl, we met a girl. Sierra blew in through a window in my heart and changed everything. She rearranged the furniture of my soul. She altered my course like a swollen river in a skinny canyon. She changed the deep darkness of my early dawn to a kaleidoscope of color exploding through crashing waves. She changed my puppy's name from Booger to Buck, and he was all grown up with the sudden confirmation. We went from two to three, and Buck and I didn't stand a chance."

"That was pretty poetic. Sounds like you've said that before."

"Yeah, I've been practicing."

"You loved her."

"Still do; we both still love her."

"Booger's still around?"

"Buck. Of course not, he's passed on too, but he still loves Sierra. She was our island of light, a beacon that we were drawn to after too many dark nights staring into the glare of oncoming headlights and sleeping under coal dark skies. I wasn't the only one that fell head over heels for Sierra, Buck did too."

"So, how did you and Buck meet Sierra?"

"We first saw her dancing in a field of clover, and I thought it was a mirage. I was running out of money and skipping meals so that Buck would have enough to eat. We got to Los Angeles, like I said, and drove straight to the beach. We walked out onto Venice Beach and fell asleep in the sun, and a cop woke me up in the middle of the night. Those waves just knocked me out. I still sleep like a log if I'm close to the ocean. Buck was curled up beside me, and the cop was poking me, and I was kind of out of it when I woke up. The guy was looking at us funny; I could tell he was trying to decide whether or not to haul us in, but I had the dog, you know, and, well, we just staggered back to the Willys and bolted."

"Sounds familiar."

"I had an aunt that lived in Santa Monica, and I found the address and we pulled up outside her house and fell back asleep and went through the whole deal again with another cop. This one was friendlier, though. We spent two nights at my aunt's—my mother's sister's house—but it was kind of strange, so I made a lame excuse and we drove up to Solvang and camped out in the woods near Los Olivos for about a week. That's when I really ran out of food."

"Sierra."

"I'm getting to that, relax."

"Hey, no rush, I just thought you lost your focus there."

"No, I'm on course, be patient. I was looking for a job."

"This is going to lead to Sierra?"

"Yeah, do you mind? I like to take my time, in case you hadn't noticed."

"I noticed."

"Sierra was at this commune. The Shy Owl Creek family they called themselves. I thought it was real cool when I stumbled upon it, but looking back now, it makes me feel kind of dirty somehow. I mean, it was dirty. Everybody was dirty, but I don't mean dirty like dirt, I mean dirty, like, I don't know. Not sexual dirty, though there was plenty of that, but just . . . no, dirty isn't the word. Forget it, there's another word, a different feeling, I don't have it right.

"It was up in the Redwoods north of San Francisco in Marin County by the Russian River. It was a beautiful spot, but of course, it wasn't theirs, and they got chased off after Sierra and I left. Buck and I stayed with those wackos for a couple of weeks, maybe a month. I was good with my hands, and I liked to work, and I was trying to impress Sierra with how tough and capable I was.

"I fell so hard for her. The moment I laid eyes on her I was in love. It was like a fire bell clanging in my head. At first I was afraid that she belonged to somebody, but she didn't. There was a lot of free loving going on, but I was real relieved to see that she wasn't part of that scene. God, I get this unbelievable feeling thinking about those first few weeks with her. She just stole my heart."

"That's beautiful."

"No, she was beautiful. She's still beautiful. She's the most beautiful person I have ever known, and I want to cry right now remembering what she looked like that first day when I walked down that dirt road, heard that music, and snuck up on the edge of that field. There were probably thirty people dancing in the bright sunlight, but I only saw her."

"Did she see you?"

"No, she had her eyes closed. That was a dumb question. Don't ruin the mood, huh?"

"Sorry, I didn't . . . excuse me."

"Yeah, me too, that was a little harsh. Sometimes that aggression jumps out. After all these years, I still bark when my train of thought gets interrupted. I'm sorry too. Where were we?"

"We were in bright sunlight . . . dancing."

"Yeah, yeah, yeah, oh man. Want to take a break?"

"No, this is getting good. I want to know what happened."

"Fine, we left."

"What?"

"Sierra, Buck, and I left."

"Okay, but before that. What happened in the field, or grove, or whatever it was? You didn't leave right away. You said . . ."

"No, we didn't leave right away. We danced first, we ate, and we slept. I worked, and made friends, and got stoned. We all got real stoned. Buck played with the other dogs. He chased the goat. We rode horses and swam in the river. I built a tree house beside the little brook they called Shy Creek, and then Sierra said she had to go, so we went."

"Where'd you go?"

"She went to France, and I went to hell."

"What?"

"Charlie Manson."

"What are you talking about?"

"That comment about going to hell made me realize what I meant when I said it was dirty. The commune had this weird edge to it—a cultish thing. That's what made me think of Charlie Manson, or Jim Jones, or David Koresh and the Branch Davidians. I'm glad we left."

"Well, what's this stuff about France?"

"Sierra went to France."

"You said that, but why?"

"She was going to the Sorbonne. It was all planned long before Buck and I came along. Of course, I didn't know that then. I was a wreck. I thought it was my fault, as usual. She wanted me to go down to meet her parents. She wanted me to come with her to Paris. She didn't want to lose me anymore than I wanted to lose her, but I couldn't see it then. It was all about me. It was always all about me. So I sulked, and I took my dog, and got in my old Willys, and left her."

"Wait a minute. Slow down, buster. Give me some detail. How did we get here so quick? Can you fill in some places for me?"

"I don't even know why I'm telling you all of this?"

"Because, you're supposed to."

"Says who?"

"Says you. You're the talker, I'm the listener. You need to talk."

"Right, okay. Sierra had spent a year at Stanford and had been accepted to a year abroad at the Sorbonne. She was just killing time at the commune when I showed up. I mean there was a lot more involved. Jem was really the one who wanted to experiment with the hippie life, but he didn't have the balls to do it by himself, so he dragged Sierra along."

"Who is Jem?"

"I didn't mean to say that he didn't have the balls. Sorry about that."

"Go on."

"He just wasn't a very independent guy, and Sierra was nothing if not independent. They were childhood friends, had grown up together in Woodside. Jem knew that Sierra was going through a rough time with her folks. He was a sensitive guy."

"Jem?"

"Yeah, Jem was a sensitive guy. Jeremiah was his real name, I think. I didn't know any of this. I didn't even know that she was with Jem at first, and then when I found out I wanted to slap him around. It wasn't like that, though. They really were just very good friends, and having Jem around was kind of protection for her, too."

"Until you showed up."

"Yeah, well, anyway, she had these plans in the works, and I just complicated things. I mean, she had the tickets and the school was paid for, and in retrospect her folks were just waiting for her to leave the country so they could dump the façade. Her old man moved down to Palm Springs as soon as her plane left California air space."

"So you and Buck left, again."

"Again."

"Familiar. I'm seeing a pattern here, aren't I?"

"You're not so dumb after all."

"Careful, buster."

"Yeah, we packed up the Willys and headed north. I was numb for a couple hundred miles. I kept driving farther and farther away from her, but my mind kept circling back into her arms. Oh, it was tough. I felt like I couldn't take a deep breath, like there was a hot coal in my chest that flamed when I sucked in air.

"We got to Eureka and cut back east through the mountains to the highway and then continued north into Oregon. That's real pretty country, man. I remember thinking that someday Sierra and I could settle down up there in the Cascades, but then it would suddenly dawn on me that I'd probably never see her again. We camped at Crater Lake for a couple of weeks, but it was starting to get cold, so I got the bright idea of going up to Mount Hood and working at the ski area."

"You were pretty sad, weren't you?"

"I was devastated. I was so broken-hearted. Thank God I had Buck . . . oh, sorry."

"Listen, you don't have to keep apologizing for your language, okay? I've heard it all, believe me. Speak in the language you're comfortable with, please. Don't worry about hurting my sensibilities."

"Right, okay, I was fucking broken-hearted, okay?"

"Yeah, okay. So did you go to Mount Hood?"

"We did, and it was good. I signed right on with the ski grooming guys. The season was just beginning, which was cool because I was kind of senior to the other ski bums. I ended up driving a big grooming cat and picked my own hours. I worked from about ten at night until eight or nine in the morning.

It was therapeutic. Buck was with me all the time. The only down side was that I lived with a bunch of party animals, but we were on totally different hours. I got to the mountain about eight at night and prepped my rig, and drank coffee with the mechanics, and then it was just me and my dog out all night under that big, beautiful Oregon sky. I was into a little bit of country at the time. It was appropriate music for my melancholy. I had this tiny cassette player and I listened to Willy Nelson, Hank Williams, and Waylon Jennings. Eight tracks were still around so I would transfer tunes from them onto the cassettes back at the house during the day when my roommates were off at work, or wherever the hell they were. Sorry, no, I mean, not sorry. I uh . . . where was I?"

"Eight tracks, so yeah, anyway."

"Anyway, I listened to Delta blues, and some sad Bonnie Raitt, Delaney and Bonnie, Boz Scaggs, Rita Coolidge, and a lot of introspective Jackson Browne. Buck and I flattened snow and chased foxes with that big old machine; real foxes I mean, not girls, like four-legged red foxes."

"Yep, I got it."

"The night sky up there was awesome. After a month or two, I started going off track and blazing my own trails. We had a list of the slopes we were supposed to groom every night, and I would get those done, and then head out of bounds to make my own little paths. I got that big rig stuck a couple times, but I could handle it. I would winch myself out of the most impossible jams. There was a lot of Chico's influence working there, now that I think back on it. First of all, I had a better idea for getting my designated work done. All the other guys would do a trail top to bottom. I got to work early and figured better ways to do things. I would do the bottom half of six or eight slopes and then work my way down from the top to finish up. It made the job faster, and more efficient. Chico would have approved. I never did a whole trail either. It seemed wrong to me somehow. I had to leave something not groomed on every slope. Not everybody likes perfect, you know?"

"This conversation has changed if you haven't noticed."

"What do you mean?"

"You enjoyed that job. It's obvious. You're more enthusiastic talking about it. It was probably a very good balm for you. Healing, wasn't it?"

"It was. I still thought about her all the time, but I had Buck, and I had solitude, and I started to experience some calm, some spirituality up there. Whenever I was hip deep in the backwoods, hooking up the winch under those bright stars in the middle of nowhere, working to get that big rig off some dangerous precipice, all alone, just me and Buck . . ."

"Yeah, it was good for you."

"I always thought that my dad would be proud of me, but first I thought that Chico would be proud of me, but before that I always thought that Sierra would be proud of me. You know what? I settled for God and Buck being proud of me. Thank God for Buck, no pun intended."

"How long did you stay in Oregon?"

"I got fired about a month before the season ended."

"What happened?"

"It wasn't that big a deal. They didn't really need the groomers anymore, and they'd let most of the crew go already. It was the backwoods stuff that got me canned. The locals started discovering my secrets, and going under the wire to look for what I had groomed the night before. Word got around and pretty soon the crazies were asking the patrols and lift attendants what I'd dressed the night before. I made some sweet tracks, man, but the mountain couldn't endorse letting stoners jump the boundary lines. They told me to quit, but of course, I didn't."

"Of course not."

"Hey, I was the one skiing them. I cut those fine trails for myself, and did a lot of backwoods skiing, just me and my trusty dog.

"Buck and I headed up to Seattle and got work on a fishing boat out of Port Townsend, but that only lasted for one trip—one very dangerous, very frightening trip. It was eleven days of terror. I was sure Buck was going to fall overboard or get hurt, so I collected my pay when we got back to shore and never looked back."

"What then?"

"We drove up to Canada, and aimed for the east coast again. Ended up in New Hampshire, and I signed on with a logging outfit. It was a beautiful drive across the mountains of Canada, but it peters out in the Plains and gets real boring after Toronto. We made Montreal and cut down through Vermont and headed over to New Hampshire. It was springtime. I was thinking about going back to work at one of the ski areas. I knew my way around the business, but the season was still six or seven months off, so I started clearing lots for a developer."

"Always working."

"Gotta eat."

"What about your family?"

"What about them?"

"Didn't you stay in touch with your parents?"

"I needed some space. I'd grown up with a lot of fear, and I was working on getting some self-esteem back. I can say that now, because I know it's true. I had no idea then, though. There was madness in that house, and today I recognize that I was part of it, but I certainly didn't back then. We were all contributors. If you're not part of the solution, you're part of the problem, right?"

"But surely you couldn't have known then . . . growing up, you didn't realize . . ."

"You know what? Our dinner table was a war zone. Everybody was walking around locked and loaded, 'cause when the bullets started flying it was every man for himself. My parents had nineteen grandchildren when they died, and every one of those kids was afraid of them. My daughter called them Grumpy and The Gramminator."

"They did the best they could."

"Hey, I know that. I'm not mad. I forgive. I was wrong a lot, too. I've made my amends, but back then I just needed some room, okay?"

"I understand. You've been tortured with shame for a very long time."

"No, really, I'm over that now. I've moved on. That stuff is all behind me. In the end I just wanted to be a positive force and help others, especially those I loved and the people that had been there for me."

"You've always wanted to be helpful. You've been a giver and a selfless person for most of your life, but you've suffered, too. That double-edged blade of guilt and pride has tormented you. You're proud of your selflessness, proud to be available, in charge, and intentional, but it confuses you. You feel guilty about doing good things for others because you question your motives. The guilt is self—destructive. The pride's intention is to destroy those close to you."

"Destroy?"

"Maybe that's a little strong. I'm sorry. You've lived with a guilty conscience primarily because you didn't ever let anyone pat you on the back. You felt like a phony, an actor. Don't deny it. It has always surprised you that you've been able to fool people so easily. It's made you feel as though you were a stage character, and that façade has created a shameful heart. But you are very genuine."

"Why, thank you."

"I'm serious. You worked hard to get down to the right size, a proper stature. Finally, your self-concern and importance has come to strike you as amusing. It's really quite refreshing."

"I think that self-esteem thing, that particular character defect is what always made me so dishonest. I used to lie about everything."

"You didn't lie. You exaggerated, and you needed to. It was necessary for you to entertain and amuse, and you never heard a story that you felt you couldn't improve. You were trying to feel better about yourself."

"That's for sure."

"So you got to New Hampshire."

"Yeah, it wasn't the Rockies, or the Cascades, or the Sierras, but it did for about a year. I worked with a chainsaw, and then I ran the grooming operation at Cannon Mountain. I lived with Buck in a cabin in the woods with no electricity. I ate brown rice, drank apple wine, and smoked home-grown skunk weed. I should have been lonely, but I wasn't. I had Buck. Buck had me. We were never apart."

"What about Sierra?"

"I dreamed about her every night."

"So you were lonely."

"I was just in love. Head over heels, think about her all the time, desperately in love. I wondered where she was and what she was doing. It's a good thing I didn't have a phone in that cabin, because I would get this ache in the middle of the night that sometimes woke me out of a dream about her, and I wanted so much to hear her voice. I would have called her a hundred times. I was like a drunk without a bottle. I had a fever, a black wire fever, and I wanted to call her and crawl through three thousand miles of telephone line to be beside her."

"Didn't you have any friends?"

"Of course I had friends. I'm a pretty sociable guy when you get right down to it. I just wanted to be alone a lot. I was close to some people at work; had a fling or two, nothing serious. I'd gotten real handy with machinery, so I spent a lot of time in the maintenance barns working on equipment with those guys. There were parties, and Buck and I were always invited. I knew a bunch of folks around the village: store clerks, that kind of thing. But when things got bad—and they did more than I like to remember—I had Buck.

"I'd roll over in my sleeping bag and pull him close to me, and just hold him tight. He held me back. I had a mattress that I'd plop down on the floor in front of the stove. I always slept in the sleeping bag. I never had any women up to the cabin, or any guys either, for that matter. That was sacred territory; just Buck and me."

"It sounds like a lonely existence."

"Well, it wasn't."

"I'm sorry I was trying to be empathetic."

"It's okay. We left in the middle of April. I didn't want to deal with mud season, and I needed some sun. I finally took the chains off the Willys and we headed south. It's funny, I'd rebuilt the engine on that old doll right before Halloween and the next day I put chains on all four tires, and they stayed on until we drove out of the valley six months later. I dropped them at the bottom of the entrance ramp to Interstate 91."

"What about your house—your cabin, I mean?"

"I don't know, I just left it; closed the door and walked out. It's not like I had to turn off the porch light. I left about a cord of split wood and two milk jugs filled with water. I was a squatter. Buck and I found the place half way up the mountain in the fall and just moved in. Nobody ever came around collecting rent. It was really a cool location with a view of the whole Presidential Range, but there were stretches of three or four weeks when the sun never came out. The gray and the clouds got depressing after awhile. The sky pushed down on me. I was used to that big western sky and plenty of bright sunshine. Man, we were looking forward to Florida again, and I guess in the back of my mind I knew I was heading back out west."

"To see Sierra?"

"Yeah, to see Sierra."

SIERRA'S LIGHT

"So, we were back on the road. My best friend and I were hungry to feel the sand in our toes. We drove practically straight through to the Florida Keys. We traveled well together. Buck loved long trips. We did our usual thing: stop every three or four hours to walk, pee, eat, and drink. Sometimes I'd tie him to his thirty foot lead and slip it around the bumper while I sacked out for a couple of hours. He always barked to let me know when there was trouble, or when it was getting dark, or getting lighter, or it was time to get moving again. I thought about stopping at Chico's to visit with them, but I had my issues, and we just kept going right on down to the bottom of the country.

"Key West was wild. I got drunk with a bunch of transvestites and drag queens on Duval Street our first night in town, and then Buck and I slept it off on the beach at Zach Taylor State Park. I woke up with a hangover, cotton-mouth, and a real bad sunburn."

"Sounds like fun."

"Was that sarcasm?"

"Yes, it was."

"Well, it was fun, but not for long. It didn't last. I just wanted some beach time, so we did the butterfly museum and Hemingway's place and boogied again. It was too hot down there to leave Buck in the truck for very long, and there wasn't ever really anything I wanted to do without him. It wasn't like he was going to go snorkeling with me, and we'd already figured out that we weren't too crazy about boats."

"Sierra was on your mind."

"There was that, of course, but at that point I hadn't seen her or spoken to her in almost twenty months."

"Almost twenty months?"

"Exactly twenty months. We cruised around the Keys for a couple of days, and finally found a cool spot to camp in Islamorada. Buck and I loved camping out under the stars, and the stars were beautiful down in the Keys. They weren't like desert stars or mountain stars, but they were a lot better than what passes for celestial entertainment in the harsh New England winter. We stayed there for a week or so and headed back to the mainland, and that's where I lost my best friend."

"Who, Buck? Oh, no, what happened?"

"I had an old high school buddy who lived in Coral Gables. He was going to Miami, too."

"Too?"

"Well, yeah, Chico was at the University of Miami. Didn't I tell you that?"

"Maybe, I don't think you did, but maybe."

"Anyway, we crashed at this guy's place. It was so long ago, I can't even remember his name. He played on our soccer team. He might have wrestled, too, but yeah, we stayed with him for a night. The next morning the three of us walked down to Matheson Hammock Beach and Buck disappeared. Wow, I remember the name of the beach, but I can't remember my old classmate's name. And then it happened. It happened so fast. One minute he was there . . . I was swimming. He was on the beach, and then . . . then he just wasn't. I . . . oh, crap."

"Are you okay?"

"Unbelievable, I still get chocked up thinking about the panic. I was so scared. I was more scared than I had ever been before. I was more scared that morning than I ever was for the rest of my life: combat, clandestine ops, capture, torture. Nothing again ever frightened me like losing Buck that day in Miami. Driving away from Sierra was heart-wrenching, but that was a decision. Losing Buck was the most helpless I'd ever felt."

"What happened?"

"I freaked out. I ran up and down the beach and out to the parking lot and all around the park calling his name. I started out calling, but it turned into screaming. People thought I was nuts. The cops showed up and tried to calm me down. I was nuts. I was crazy. I looked everywhere for him. I still don't know what happened. It was so fast. The sun went down, and I wouldn't leave. They tried to get me to go back to my friend's apartment, but I just kept running and running. I became hoarse and couldn't call his name anymore, but I didn't stop. I was soaking wet. I was still in my bathing suit. I was still barefoot hours after he'd disappeared. I kept expanding my search in ever-widening circles, and then I'd circle back to the beach. I thought he'd been kidnapped. I thought he'd been hit by a car. I thought he'd gone in the surf after me and drowned. Everybody left. I was all alone, and I couldn't stop. I finally collapsed where my shirt and shoes were and just cried and cried. First I'd lost Sierra, and then I'd lost Buck. I considered walking into the ocean and ending it all, but I guess I fell asleep in the sand.

"I woke up hoping it was all a terrible nightmare. A tractor was dragging the beach, and the sun was just coming up over the water. He still wasn't there, and I wandered aimlessly until mid-day when my friend led me back to his place. I collapsed on the couch. I was hungry, sore, sunburned, and so terribly sad. When I woke up again I went to the police station and then the pound. I drove to the local animal shelters and filed reports everywhere. I made up leaflets with his picture on them. The only picture I had was one that Jem had taken of him as a puppy over a year and a half ago. He was in Sierra's lap with a big, happy puppy smile on his face. I searched and searched and asked everybody I saw. Eventually I moved into a motel room. I was driving my old school buddy crazy, but I kept looking. I went to the pound and the shelters every day. The people that worked in those sad places would see me coming and stop talking. I felt like some sort of pariah. I couldn't take it anymore. Finally, after five solid weeks of searching, I gave up. I hated myself for years for giving up on him."

"So what happened?"

"Well, I left Miami. I drove across the Everglades again; followed the same route Buck and I had taken when he was still Booger. I kept searching the road for him thinking I'd find his dead body somewhere along the way. I hit the Gulf and turned north up through the Florida panhandle. I didn't realize it then, but I was on my way back to California."

"Going back to Sierra, right?"

"I needed to see Sierra again. I needed to hold her and tell her that I loved her. I needed to tell her I'd lost the dog. I just couldn't face not having her and not having Buck either."

"So, you drove all the way to San Francisco?"

"Not exactly, first I joined the Navy."

"You what?"

"Yeah, it was crazy. I was driving along on Interstate 10 feeling sorry for myself when I got to Pensacola. I saw a sign for the Naval Air Base there, and for some reason, I just took the exit and drove onto the base. I pulled up at the gate and told the guard I wanted to sign up. He took my license number and directed me to the recruiter's office, and I walked in and joined the Navy. I wasn't thinking too clearly."

"No, I guess you weren't."

"I told the guy I wanted to fly jets off of aircraft carriers, and he smiled and told me that was great, sign this, and sign that, and report the next morning for a physical. It was already pretty late in the day, but this liar assured me that I'd be a naval pilot, so I said I'd be back in the morning."

"What in the world possessed you to join the Navy?"

"I don't know. I wanted to kill somebody, anybody. I think I pretty much had a death wish at that point, but hey, I really did want to learn how to fly."

"And did you?"

"Not on Uncle Sam's dime, but I did later, on my own; not jets, though."

"Okay, so you're despondent. You've lost your girl, lost your dog, and now you've joined the Navy."

"Not so fast, first I called home, but yeah, I was pretty distraught."

"That was a good idea. Your parents were probably worried about you."

"I thought you knew about this kind of stuff."

"What kind of stuff?"

"Aren't you supposed to know a little more about me, about my family? You obviously don't have the inside track on my mother and father. They were not the least bit worried about me."

"That's a terrible thing to say."

"No, it isn't. It's the truth. I had called home about six months before then just to check in. My mother acted like I was bothering her. I hadn't spoken to her in practically a year. It was right after Buck and I moved into the cabin in New Hampshire. She sounded like she thought I'd gone out to get a loaf of bread and forgot the money or something."

"I'm sorry to hear that, but it was thoughtful of you to call, anyway. Despite what you think, I'm certain they were concerned."

"Right, I asked to talk to Dad, but she said he was watching the Sunday morning political talk shows, and he would be angry if she interrupted him. They went to church every Sunday, and then he came home and screamed at the television—nice life. That kind of hypocrisy was what drove me away from home in the first place. Well, not the only thing."

"I'm sorry."

"That's not the point. The point is I was about to hang up . . . I'd told her that I was joining the Navy, and I could feel her shrug, but I was saying goodbye when she asked me if I'd spoken to Chico. She said that he had called a couple of weeks ago looking for me, because he had my dog."

"Wow."

"I jumped back in the car and drove straight through to Coconut Grove, and there he was. I ran up the steps to Billy's and Chico's apartment calling his name, and he started barking madly, and scratching the door and Billy opened it, and he burst into my arms . . . oh, man that was happy. He was whining and whimpering. I was crying and hugging him. He was licking me, and I was kissing him and holding him. I promised that I'd never let him go again . . . but of course, I did."

"Why?"

"I had to. I'd enlisted, remember? I didn't show up for my physical the next day obviously, but I had made a commitment to those people. Believe me, at the time I had no intention of honoring it, but eventually Sierra made me go back."

"To Pensacola? To the Navy?"

"No, San Diego."

"You've lost me."

"Really, aren't you supposed to know all of this?"

"No, I'm not. Forget your expectations, and tell me the story."

"Okay, I was a skinny, dirty, raggedy looking nineteen-year-old kid. I'd just driven onto the base in an old Willys truck that predated me by thirty years. I had a pony-tail I could sit on. I was wearing a Bob Marley T-shirt and ripped jeans. I'd been bathing in the ocean for a month or two and hadn't shaved in even longer. Would you have expected me to show up the next day?"

"Sure."

"Really? Come on, the last thing the recruiter had told me was that they'd initiate a criminal background check on me so that it would be complete by the time I reported back the next day for my physical. If I was that guy, I'd have never expected to see me again."

"So what happened?"

"The same thing that always happened to me—Sierra."

"She made you go back?"

"Uh huh, except we were in California, and it was three weeks later. I walked onto the Navy base in San Diego thinking we'd all get a good chuckle out of it and that they'd tell me it was okay. I figured it happened all the time; guys change their minds, right?"

"Didn't happen?"

"Nope, they gave me a physical and told me to report for basic training in eleven days. I was in the United States Navy."

"Tell me about hooking up with Sierra again."

"You bet. That's the best part. Buck and I drove to Palo Alto, well, Woodside was technically where her folks lived. It was right on the border. We took about three days, drove pretty much straight through. I was convinced that I loved her, and I couldn't stand not knowing how she felt about me."

"Did you call first?"

"No, I was afraid to. I wasn't even sure she was home. She could have still been in Paris for all I knew, but I had to settle things in my mind. I knew there had been trouble at home with her parents, but I didn't know that they'd actually split up. The whole preconceived scenario that I'd been dreaming up couldn't have been more wrong."

"Why? Her parents had separated? You know preconceptions practically never pan out."

"Oh, yeah, but it was a lot more than that. First of all, I had no idea how rich she was. I mean, I knew that she'd gone to a private school, and that she'd started college at Stanford, but I had no idea that she was the daughter of rich people. I mean very, very rich people. Heck, I'd met her on a hippie commune."

"Go on."

"Well, I know now that she was at Shy Creek to sort of escape from the craziness of her household. She was an only child, you know, and of course, she blamed herself for the divorce. Going to Paris was more about escape and denial that the whole drama was going down."

"It must have been very difficult for her."

"I think you're right, and that's probably why she kept the baby."

"What baby?"

"Asia, her baby, our baby, she had our daughter."

"Whoa, she had your baby?"

"Okay, I really don't get it. How do you not know this?"

"Look, I tried to tell you . . . never mind, just tell me the rest."

"Am I shaking my head right now?"

"Yes."

"Good, okay, I'm not nuts. We got to her house, Buck and I. Are you with me? I guess it was her mother's house by then. Her old man had left. First of all, I was road weary as heck, Buck was too, and we were cruising through this incredibly fancy neighborhood. Woodside is beautiful. I can't remember how I got the address; Sierra must have given it to me sometime. I couldn't see any of the houses from the road, but I finally found the mailbox. I turned down this lush driveway that was like a trail through the rainforest. It suddenly opened up to a beautiful lawn climbing a little hill to a Spanish style stucco ranch house sitting on a knoll. It wasn't a real big house, it seemed to blend into the landscape, but it spread out from the front door in both directions and from the circular drive I couldn't see either end of the place. So, it seemed big, but it really wasn't.

"There was a little Asian lady wearing a floppy straw hat at the bottom of the hill where the driveway split. She was on her knees in one of the flower beds. That was Shushu. There were two Mexican guys cutting the grass with old-fashioned manual push-mowers. There were two other guys on the roof re-pointing the chimney, and there was a guy walking around toward the back with a pool brush over his shoulder and a canvas bag in his other hand. Even after all these years I dream of that scene, the scene I saw the first time I drove up to Sierra's house."

"It sounds beautiful."

"It was magical, and I felt invisible. It was very quiet, and nobody even looked up at me. I had put a new exhaust on the Willys and it was loud. I knew it was loud. I liked that, but nobody even turned toward us. I suddenly wanted to shave, shower, cut my hair, brush my teeth, and put on a seersucker suit. For a second, I thought I might be able to back down through the rainforest and start over, but I was committed."

"You never backed down from anything."

"See, you know that kind of stuff, but you don't know about my parents or my daughter. How can that be?"

"You're right, I know you. You are here now. We are talking about you."

"Yeah, right, we're talking about me. Know what? I'm going to just ignore the riddles and tell the goddamn story. Oh, shit, I'm sorry."

"Go on."

"There was a little parking place at the top of the circle in front of the main door. I pulled in there, walked up to the door, turned around, and looked out over the trees and bushes to the most gorgeous view of the ocean a couple of miles to the west. Shushu had stopped digging and was pulling off her gloves looking at me when the door opened silently. I felt a warm rush of air, a real pleasant, soft breeze on my back. I turned around to find one of the most striking women I had ever met. She had a lovely smile on her face and she was holding the sweetest little baby girl in the world."

"Asia?"

"Anastasia Marguerite Monroe, my baby."

"That must have been a surprise."

"Everything was a surprise. I knew it was Sierra's mother because she looked like a forty-year-old Sierra, but the house, the yard, the view, the day, and especially the baby left me a little dizzy. I didn't know that she was my child, of course, but then again something about her, something about that woman's smile, something in the air, just . . ."

"You knew she was yours."

"Yeah, I think I did. She reached out to me with those chubby, little baby arms, and to my surprise Shushu stepped between us, and Asia climbed onto her like a monkey. It took me a minute to get my bearings. I stammered, and looked from Shushu to my mother-in-law, and the whole time Sierra's mother just smiled so kindly at me and stared so deeply into my soul. I have to admit, she spooked me."

"You've been spooked before."

"I've been spooked plenty, but I've never been so spooked that I couldn't move, and that's the way I was when Sierra flew out the door right past me screaming Buck's name."

"That's great."

"She never even acknowledged me. She took the steps in a leap, and ran to the truck, and I could hear Buck's tail thumping on the seat. Sierra yanked the door open, I thought it might come right off in her hand, and Buck exploded into her arms. Cheez, what a great memory; I've had that image burned in my brain for forty years."

"What did you do?"

"I introduced myself. I've always been polite. Sierra's mom nodded and said that she knew who I was. She said she'd been expecting me, that Sierra wasn't so sure, but that she knew I'd feel the tug and show up."

"The tug?"

"That's what she said. I asked the same thing. I asked her what that meant. She just smiled and said that the baby had my ears. I thought the baby was hers. Well, not really, but she didn't look very old to me. Heck, Asia could have been hers. Like I said, I don't think she was even forty-years-old the day I met her. She was looking right into my heart, man, like she instantly knew everything about me. I loved her right away."

"You loved Sierra's mother?"

"Yes, I mean, no, not like that, but of course I loved her. I still love her. She's special. She's an ancient, an old soul. I never could figure out why Sierra's father left that woman."

"Maybe she intimidated him."

"Nah, he was a pretty tough guy himself. It wasn't another woman either; although it didn't take him long to find someone else after he moved to Palm Springs. I don't know what happened, why they split up. They were always cordial to one another. I think they always loved each other. Maybe it was just that they both had such overpowering personalities. Sierra got their strength too, but it hurt her badly when they separated."

"She said the baby had your ears?"

"Come on, don't laugh. I knew she couldn't tell at ten months—or however old Asia was—whether she had my ears or not. She knew too. She was just trying to be polite. She was reaching out in her own way, looking for a connection. We all look for a connection, don't we? I think that's primarily what life is all about, finding a connection with another human being. It's about relationships. I was standing on her porch, and she was trying to tie us together somehow. It broke the ice."

"Okay, so you're standing on her porch . . ."

"Uh huh, Sierra was cavorting with Buck. I'd never seen him so happy. They were literally rolling around on the ground together. She was on her knees with her back to us and she was growling at Buck and he was lunging at her and running around tearing up that beautiful lawn. He'd come back to face her, and they'd stare each other down, and then he'd tear around again.

"Asia was squealing and Sierra's mother, Shushu, and I were laughing. Sierra suddenly seemed to make a decision. She got up off her knees with her back still turned toward us, squared her shoulders, looked out over the trees, and finally turned and faced me, well us, but she was staring at me."

"This sounds very dramatic."

"Oh, yeah, that girl was dramatic. She got it from her mother and passed it along to our little girl. She walked up to us. Shushu handed the baby to me, and Sierra said, 'I see you've met your daughter.'"

"Whew, very dramatic."

"Like the sky was going to explode, and the earth was going to crack open, and Charlton Heston was going to charge up the driveway on the back of a lion. I said nothing. I just looked miles into those deep, intense eyes of hers and didn't say a word. She said that she didn't think that she would ever see me again, and then she cried. And then her mother cried, and Shushu cried, and I could feel myself choking up, but then that little baby reached up and grabbed my bottom lip. She squeezed it really hard, I remember this so vividly, and then she squealed like a banshee."

"This is great. I don't mean to keep saying that, but I hear a lot of stories, and, well, this is just really good."

"That lightened the mood. We all started laughing, and the next thing you know, we were all hugging, squeezing Asia in between us. Shushu had her face buried in my solar plexus and when she pulled away my shirt was wet from her tears. I looked into Sierra's bottomless eyes, and there were tears in there from a million years ago, and she mouthed, 'I love you,' and pressed my face between her hands. I suddenly realized that I hadn't felt any genuine affection from another human in almost two years, since the last time I was with Sierra. I vowed to myself that I was never going to leave her again."

"But you did."

"Yeah, I sure did."

"Then what happened?"

"She took my hand, and she took the baby, and then we started walking around the side of the house. Buck was right on our heels wagging his tail like a windmill. He was making doggie noises, whining and cooing, and Asia couldn't keep her eyes off of him. She was crawling over her mother's shoulder to look at him, and she was laughing and giggling. They didn't have a dog in that house; plenty of cats though. Buck spent way too much time chasing cats, and that didn't make him real popular with Shushu, but nobody else minded. He wouldn't have hurt any of them.

"I tried to talk. I tried to say that I was sorry, but she just kept pulling me around to the back of the house. The guys in the yard and the guys on the roof had stopped working. They were all staring at us, and when we got into the back, the pool guy quit working, and he stared at us too. I don't know, maybe that was just my impression. It was like the world stopped. I mean ten minutes earlier it was just me and my dog. All of a sudden, I was a family."

"This is wonderful."

"Yeah, well, I wasn't so sure. Sierra led me to a break in the hedgerow that I would never have noticed. The yard was like a little park. It was like entering another world, a magical fairy land with mulch paths, and exotic plants, and little statues, birdfeeders, figurines, even a grape arbor, and a tiny pond. It had kind of a Japanese neatness, an Asian kind of compactness to it. This, I later found out, was Shushu's world. Maybe she was the one that chased Sierra's father out of there. I don't know."

"I wouldn't be surprised. She sounds like a very strong personality too."

"You got that right. Anyway, we sat down on a bamboo bench beside a fat, little Buddha, and I just listened to her talk. I was tired, and her words were soft and soothing. I watched them float on the air like light motes, translucent little light motes. Buck plopped down too, like he was totally and finally content to just listen to Sierra's voice. We both loved the sound of her voice. I have no idea what she said. I don't recall a thing, but I just let her talk. We all have to be listened to. We all have to be heard, or at least we have to think that we're being heard."

"Did you know that then?"

"I think I did. Actually I do remember what she was talking about, not exactly, but in a general way, you know? It was just her story. How she got to Paris and realized that she was pregnant, and how frightened she was. We weren't even twenty-years-old yet. She talked about how sad she was to have left me, but that she knew she had to. When she got to France she was lonely, and then she realized that she was carrying a part of me inside her, and she was ecstatic but scared too, I guess. But thrilled, and suddenly not so lonely, which makes sense. She really just needed to get it all out, and she hadn't had a chance to do that yet; not safely, anyway."

"Yes, we need to be heard."

"I think that was probably the first time in my life that I realized how important it is to be present for somebody else. I learned what it means to practice the art of listening, being patient, tolerant, and considerate of another person. I learned to be quiet and to just be there to allow another traveler the opportunity to express their feelings. Like I said, I watched her words. They came out of her mouth and floated. Did I say that?"

"You said they looked like motes."

"Yeah, light motes, and those soft little white dandelion seeds, the hairs, the parachute things, you know?"

"The pappus."

"What?"

"The little white, floaty, fluff ball hairs are called pappus."

"Well, that's what her words looked like to me; floating gently on the wind, swirling around us. This happy, gurgling, beautiful little baby sat on her lap playing with her mommy's hair, and the dandelion seed-words floated all around us. I was trying to grasp that this baby was mine. At that moment I thought that I might lose them both, that Sierra would suddenly tell me to leave and never come back. I realized how much that frightened me, and that I cared more about these two special creatures than I had ever cared about myself, or anything else for that matter. There had been Buck of course, but on a different level. I never really cared that much about me before. I didn't have a lot of self-worth. You know that golden rule prayer? Of course you do; *Help me to do unto others as I would* blah, blah, blah. I always finished it; *Help me to do unto others better than I would ever expect others to do unto me.* I just wasn't raised to think that I was very important."

"That's terrible."

"Not really, but I decided then and there that if Sierra wanted me to stay with her, I sure wasn't going to ever let my baby think that she wasn't the most important thing in the world."

"You had your priorities straight."

"I'm not so sure about that. She had hers straight though. I think she struggled with being pregnant early on. She was young, had her whole life ahead of her, and newly arrived in the City of Light. I'm sure there were plenty of doctors in the Latin Quarter that would have eliminated her little problem for her. Then she could have gotten back to being an avant-garde art student. Thank God for Marguerite."

"Who's Marguerite?"

"Marguerite was her roommate. I don't want to give you the impression that Sierra was actually considering abortion, I doubt that she was, but Marguerite was there for her. She was her confidante, her best friend, and ultimately, her labor coach. Marguerite was present, you know? She told Sierra that having Asia was her destiny, and then she supported her through nine months of pregnancy."

"That was a heck of a commitment for a pair of art students."

"No kidding. Don't interrupt me, please. Sitting on that little bench in Shushu's garden that day, Sierra made me understand that. She made me realize that this was meant to be. She told me that this little baby was her light. The sun was piercing shafts of brilliance through the trees like arrows and spears, and she said that Asia was her light. I was her love, but Asia was her light. She said that she knew she couldn't live without her light and her love.

"When she arrived at the San Francisco Airport with that little bundle of joy in her arms it changed her relationship with her mother forever. She said the tension was gone. That reunion was the beginning of a new understanding between the two of them, and Sierra realized at that moment how hard and judgmental she had been to her parents. She said that she was able to finally forgive them for the hard choices they had made."

"This is really good stuff."

"I was scared in so many ways that I couldn't recognize then. I felt like such an intruder. You have to understand how much of a female world this appeared to be to me. I didn't feel like I belonged, and like I said before, I was kind of expecting to be told to leave."

"But that didn't happen."

"No, they welcomed me. They drew me in and assured me that I was meant to be a part of this."

"You were the father."

"I believe I still am. Boy, it feels good to talk like this. It's cathartic. I needed to get this off my chest. There's a lot I've been holding back for a very long time."

"So, you fell in love with her again."

"I never fell out of love. I only wish I could have spent more time with her. We stayed with her mom for about a week before I finally let Sierra talk me into contacting the Navy. I didn't really care about any enlistment or promise that I'd made, but she was trying to get me to be responsible about it. We decided that we'd take a weekend up in the Redwoods and then drive down the coast to San Diego and I could check in with the powers-that-be there. It was a good plan, except I ended up in the Navy for the rest of my life."

"Really? You weren't really in the Navy for the rest of your life, were you?"

"Well, not technically, but I guess you wouldn't get the subtlety. How much of this story do you know, and how much are you pretending you don't know? Never mind, it doesn't matter. Anyway, the three of us drove back up to Shy Creek. The hippies were gone—chased off, I guess. The only trace of the commune was a black hole in the field where they used to have the bonfires. That was appropriate, right? We found the tree house I'd built two summers before, swept it out, and slept in it for a couple of nights. The place was totally different with just us. It was heaven: two happy kids, a beautiful little baby, a gorgeous spot in the California wilderness. Man, I hated to leave."

"The drive down the coast must have been nice, though."

"Oh, yeah, I'd done it a couple of times by then, but it never gets old. We took our time and stopped in Monterey, spent the night in Carmel, had lunch at Nepenthe in Big Sur, spent the next night in Santa Barbara . . . it was fun, and then we got to San Diego."

"Were you in trouble?"

"Not really, they called Pensacola and confirmed what I'd told them and then they said that they weren't starting another boot camp for eleven more days. I took my physical. We drove out to Palm Springs where I met the old man, and eventually I asked him for permission to marry his daughter."

"How'd that go?"

"Great. He said, 'No.'"

DUTY

"Boot camp was kind of a breeze for me."

"Wait a minute. What happened in Palm Springs? What did Sierra's father say to you? When did you get married, I mean, how did you get married? What about . . ."

"Hey, one thing at a time, I'll get to all of that. Listen to me for a minute, please. Okay?"

"Sure, but I just want to make sure you don't skip over anything important. That's pretty much the purpose of this whole exercise."

"There's a purpose to this? This conversation is some sort of exercise?"

"Now who's asking the questions?"

"Good point. So, boot camp was a breeze, got it? Yeah, you do. It was a breeze because I was in much better shape than most of the other recruits. I had been raised by a tough Scotsman who had served some perilous duty under very difficult conditions in Korea, and he never let me forget it. I wasn't afraid of hard work. I'd been tested, and I knew something about physical and mental deprivation. I knew how to take orders, and I didn't take crap from anybody that I didn't have to. I was a tough kid, so camp flew by for me.

"Nixon had just rescinded the draft, and the Navy wasn't being inundated by guys trying to avoid the Army and the jungles of Vietnam anymore. The Paris Peace Accords had been signed. Nixon had reduced troop strength by over seventy percent, and America was actually starting to win the war. I'm not sure how that happened exactly, but it was like Congress quit trying to micro-manage the thing for awhile, and the President unleashed a bombing campaign that was being directed by professional soldiers instead of politicians. Somehow all of that added up to a boot camp with a bunch of momma's boys.

There really weren't any first-rate sailors signing commitment letters all of a sudden. I didn't care. I was going to fly F-4 Phantoms anyway."

"So why didn't that ever happen?"

"I flunked the physical."

"You flunked the physical?"

"That's what I said. Don't act so surprised. The downside was that they didn't tell me until ten weeks into basic, and I had been bragging to all the other guys that I was going to be a pilot. That really wasn't so important, but it was the Friday before our first weekend leave. Sierra and the baby had driven out from the desert to visit, and I was sure Sierra was going to be disappointed."

"Was she?"

"Of course not, she was delighted that I wasn't going to fly kamikaze off an aircraft carrier, but that wasn't what I expected. I wanted to be a hero for her. I wanted to impress her. It seemed to me, at the time, that I was just disappointing another person that was important to me. That had become a pattern in my life. I'd spent my whole life feeling like I could never live up to other people's expectations. It wasn't until years later that I realized that I was the only guy expecting any grand and wonderful accomplishments."

"Who did you assume had these expectations of you?"

"You know the answer to that—my father, of course. The Navy gave me the self esteem to face the fact that he never really cared one way or the other. And I was okay with that, but I still wanted to do the right thing. I wanted to succeed. I wanted to be famous—no, not famous, but dependable, and that was tough early on."

"What did they flunk you for?"

"My eyes. I couldn't see well enough to fly Navy jets. Oh, my eyesight wasn't real bad, but they don't waste a million bucks training guys unless their eyes are perfect, and I guess mine weren't. I could see well enough to qualify for sniper training. I could hit a curve ball, you know? But after all that running and all those push-ups, I was told that I was going to be just another E-1, Seaman Recruit. That was okay, because you know what? We worship our fantasies, and I had no way of knowing then that it would work out the way it did. Sometimes I think of progress as just being afraid to look back, and I didn't appreciate then that I was learning how to be a man. In the end, the riddles of life always seem to be more satisfying than the solutions."

"So where did you end up?"

"Well, that weekend I ended up in a motel room right outside the base with my fiancée and my baby."

"Still not married?"

"Nope, and not getting much closer either. I was sure she was going to dump me. I was sending her my pay, but it was pathetic. We got paid monthly, and I think my first check was for about $200. I had made more working for my old man when I was in high school. I knew pilots made the big money, but I was so disappointed when I had to tell her that I was just going to be another swabbie on a tin bucket. Sierra didn't care, though. She was happy. Her folks were taking care of her. Both of her parents adored the baby. She promised me that she'd wait, but like I said, I was having my doubts."

"She was living with her father then?"

"Yeah, pretty much, I guess. I think she was back and forth a lot. She spent my deployment with her mother. That's where I sent my letters, anyway."

"Did you write to her a lot?"

"Every day. That's the only thing I spent money on—stamps. Sierra sent me a box of stationery and envelopes, and I mailed a letter to her each night. They didn't go anywhere until the censors cleared them and the mail drop picked them up. That was pretty irregular when we were at sea, but I still wrote every night. After I saw all the deductions out of that first tiny paycheck, I quit buying anything but stamps. Heck, I thought the Navy should have paid for those, too."

"I thought the United States military was the highest paid army in the world."

"We were, but I was in the Navy, by the way. It was the mid-seventies. We made minimum wage as Seamen Recruits and E-1's. That's why I wanted to fly jets, well, that was one of the reasons. I thought the fly boys were rich, and compared to us, they were. We shipped out of Diego for maneuvers and training with the Brits. I was on one of the Tenders, and we were escorting a Destroyer in the Carrier Group. We sailed through the Canal, across the Atlantic, and into the Med. The Carrier and the rest of the Battle Group went around the Horn, but we were supposed to pick up a detachment of sailors in the Gulf of Mexico, so we went through Panama before rejoining the rest of the Group. That's when I first ran into Navy SEALS. They were out of Pensacola, and they landed in an AH-60 on the Destroyer we were shadowing. We eventually dropped anchor in the Azores before entering the Mediterranean, and that's where I decided that I wanted to be a SEAL."

"What's a SEAL?"

"Special operations forces of the Navy, specializing in unconventional warfare. It stands for Sea, Air, and Land teams. 'The only easy day was yesterday'."

"Is that the motto?"

"It's one of them.

"So, what's so great about being one of those guys?"

"First of all, it paid more, and I really wanted to be able to send more money back to Sierra and the baby. More importantly, though, it appealed to my sense of adventure. When we picked up the east coast team, I thought they were just a bunch of highly trained explosives guys, but they ran a training insert in the Azores that really impressed me. I saw a lot of what was going on in that first deployment because I volunteered for whatever my Petty Officer needed. Some sailors don't stick their heads up for anything; I was the opposite."

"You volunteered a lot?"

"I volunteered for everything. Ship duty is boring, and I'm just naturally curious. I delivered mail, painted torpedo hangars, fixed busted toilets, ran messages to the brass, served hors d'oeuvres to the Captain, walked the C.P.O.'s dog."

"Somebody had a dog?"

"Yeah, our Chief Petty Officer had a little rat toy poodle that he smuggled on board. I went everywhere and saw everything. I was on every ship in the Carrier Group. I flew gun crew on helicopters, and pulled watch on the Transports, but the night I saw the SEAL teams go into Horta and capture the Fayal Hotel did it for me. I wanted to be one of them."

"Your Navy captured a hotel?"

"It was a drill, an exercise. I was with them on the Sea Knight. It was pretty crowded—both teams, a spotter, a gunner, and the pilots. I was assigned to help the SEALs with their gear. They carry a ton of stuff into a mission. I later found out that they generally walk or swim out with nothing but their weapons and hopefully a couple rounds of ammo left."

"What's a Sea Knight?"

"It's funny, the Navy was always all about rules and regulations and discipline. That's what I loved about it. The discipline was a stabilizing force in my life. Knowing that there was a rule for everything, and that every action had a procedure was important. I never had that growing up, and it reassured me. But when it came to putting SEALs into a Huey, all the rules went out the window. Every aircraft has a weight restriction. That law is rigorously enforced, especially on a Carrier where safety trumps everything. There is never supposed to be any deviation from procedure, but we always overloaded those choppers—not the attack ships, not the AH 46's, but those UH transports got weighted down, man. I mean, when it came to extraction that was understandable. If you're trying to get guys out of a hot zone, under fire, weight wasn't really a concern. As long as those big, floppy rotors could pull that thing into the air, the more bodies you could squeeze in, the better off you were. Nothing else mattered. I don't know. I was just always amazed when we loaded those Knights up going into action. I couldn't understand why we didn't just requisition another bird."

"What's a Sea Knight?"

"Sorry. I heard you the first time. It's a CH-46E helicopter. On that first mission, I watched those sailors as they dropped out of the chopper into the pitch black ocean with all kinds of gear. I could barely make out the inflatables as they started paddling to shore. We were probably about five miles out, so those rafts came in handy. Jumping out of choppers became routine for me, but I sure was impressed the first time I saw a pair of SEAL Teams pull that maneuver. I loved the feeling of kicking myself loose from the earth, and I loved the feeling of jumping out of aircraft. Falling always felt like flying to me."

"There's a message in there somewhere."

"Yeah, I think you're right. For me, it was almost an unconscious act; the pre-rational instinct of an unrehearsed life, you might say."

"Before you turn to something else, can we get caught up with Sierra and the little one? Where are they? What were your intentions? You were back with her briefly. You discovered you shared a baby. You told me how much you loved her. What was going on?"

"Man, you're always on Sierra."

"Well, I think that's where you're headed. That's what's really going on with you."

"You're right, of course. Sierra is the essence, but my thoughts are on the duty right now. I love my work. I love my country. Those two things are my passions, different from Sierra, though. There was always something much deeper with her. She stirred a different kind of ardor and infatuation within me, especially over time. When we were finally able to spend more uninterrupted time together, able to start growing together . . ."

"When was that?"

"After my injuries, I was rotated out, and we started developing as a couple, as a team. There began to be a sense, a feeling of complete satisfaction inside of me when I was with her after a while, like my soul was breathing a deep sigh of relief and comfort. It was as if there was a beautiful,

58

gushing fountain within me waiting to be discovered, and she found it. Sierra filled me. We became a knot that couldn't be untied. None of that started to develop though, until I was out of the game, and back in her world. So, I'll get there, okay?"

"Good."

"Yeah, good. So we sailed into the Mediterranean and were chopped to Sixth Fleet. Once we joined the Carrier Battle Group, we had over forty ships with four separate SEAL Teams—two from the east coast and two from the west. They were then assigned to Task Force 64 Special Operations and continued carrying out search and destroy, and boarding and capturing drills and exercises. By then my Petty Officer knew I wanted to be a part of the action, so I participated in all the drops and insertions as the donkey. I was pretty much a water boy lugging gear—cleaning equipment, policing boats and aircraft. It was great."

"I'm sorry, but this is a very odd language you're speaking."

"I can make it easier. We stayed in the Med for seven weeks of war games. We only had one liberty leave. Sixth Fleet is based in Naples, so that was where the passes were issued. I was still officially assigned to a Tender tasked to a Destroyer. We were the last into Naples. Most of our guys hit the first waterfront bar and stayed there for the next seventy-two hours. Not me. I traveled as far and as fast as I could. I hopped a train to Rome and then onto Tuscany. I wanted to go to Venice, but I started running out of time, and Tuscany blew me away anyhow. I crammed as much sight-seeing into three days as possible and found out that I loved Italy. I arrived back on board, sober and on-time, so they made me a temporary S.P. and sent me back to Naples to round up the drunks."

"S.P.?"

"Shore Patrol, I was a cop with a badge and a stick. No gun, though. Naples has been the home base of Sixth since the end of World War II, so they were used to drunken sailors. We got everybody back on deck—I think we left about thirty sailors and marines in Italian jails—and we sailed for home. My P.O. approached me on the trip back to San Diego about applying for SEAL school, and the deal was done. He ran it up to the Chief who recommended me for the duty, and when we got back to base I got my orders. I went to Coronado for S.B.I. and . . ."

"S.B.I.?"

"Seal Basic Indoctrination. I went through the initial Navy SEAL program in three weeks and then I had ten days off with Sierra and the baby. Back to Coronado for ten more weeks of general training, and then another ten days off. Eight more weeks of diving, followed by nine weeks of land warfare up in the Cuyamaca Mountains, and finally three weeks of parachuting, and then I got my Trident. Basic was everything; weapons, tactics, equipment, survival techniques, demolition training, communications, and a whole lot of swimming."

"What's a Trident?"

"That's what SEALS get when they become SEALs; a gold Navy SEAL Trident pin. I still can't believe I ended up a SEAL. I wanted to fly jets. I didn't like to swim, and brother, we swam a lot. We swam for hours. We swam for days. They tried to freakin' drown us, but I loved it. I loved basic training, loved living in a barracks with other guys, and loved the discipline and camaraderie. I loved being in shape, running, shooting, the obstacle course, the mountains, everything about it, but I did not love swimming. I liked having my own space and my own responsibilities. I'm obsessive as hell—you know that—and the Navy is a great place to be a compulsive neat freak. I missed my little family, but I qualified R.O.T. and U.D.T. I was cold as a capitalist with the M-16, AR-15, M-4, and Beretta M-9."

"I don't even want to ask."

"I was a radio operator, an underwater demolitions expert, and finally got my E.O.D. 2 which means Explosive Ordnance Disposal, 2nd Class. I was assigned to a Navy SEAL platoon and garrisoned in Coronado with Teams 1, 3, 5, and 7."

"Well, I'm glad to hear you missed your wife while you were having all this fun."

"Yeah, but it worked out okay. Looking back on it now, I really believe that everything worked out the way it was supposed to. Being away from each other made everything better when we were together. I ached from missing her, but I thought about her and the baby all the time. In a way, that was what got me through some of the toughest days of training. I would dream about the three of us living in a cabin that I had built with my own hands. We would be somewhere up in the Redwoods, away from it all, yet close enough to some cute, little hip town. Asia would be our focus, our main concern—heck that wasn't a dream—that became reality. She would be woven into the fabric of our happy life together. We would be like three chocolate bars on a hot summer day, melted down and all run together."

"Did you tell Sierra that you dreamed these dreams?"

"All the time—I wrote to her incessantly. She later told me that she had to read my letters alone, because they made her blush until her ears turned red. It all came true though, I mean the feelings and the love part of the fantasy."

"That's sweet."

"I want to be buried at Fort Rosecrans National Cemetery in San Diego. We used to walk around there on my leaves. We'd lay out a blanket and look out over Point Loma and the Pacific. Asia would run through the neat rows of tombstones, squealing with delight. We never worried about her getting hurt because it was so meticulously groomed and cared for. People would be there praying and putting flowers on stones and this wild little redhead would tear past them, and they would always smile. No matter how sad or solemn they were, they always smiled at little Asia. I want to be there so somebody else's baby can make Sierra and Anastasia smile when they come to visit me."

"That's nice. Does Sierra know this?"

"Uh huh, it's in my will."

"Okay, I'm warming up to this Navy stuff."

"We were involved with a lot of stuff that nobody was supposed to know about my first couple years. Right off the bat, they were sending Teams over to Angola in 1978, then El Salvador to assist and advise the FMLN in '80. We were in Nicaragua in '82 teaching the Contras how to shoot straight, but it wasn't until Grenada in '83 that we were official and legal."

"What do you mean, 'nobody was supposed to know about'?"

"We weren't officially in those disputes. We actually never got off the boat for Angola. We were about ten miles off-shore, just over the horizon from Luanda, chomping at the bit while the Commies were helping the rebels slaughter people. El Salvador was weird because we landed with the Red Cross and were unloading food and medicine at one end of a runway while Russian soldiers were unloading guns and ammo at the other end. We were wearing Red Cross uniforms, but we were armed to the teeth. Nicaragua was a sham. We were actually in-country with the Contras when the whole arms—for-hostages scam blew up. We hightailed back to Tampa pronto. We had two Teams in Iran at the time, too. They were ready to move on the bad guys when the media caught wind of everything."

"Where was Buck while you were playing soldier? You haven't mentioned him."

"Sailor, sir, I was a sailor, and Buck was with Sierra, never left her side. He traveled with her and the baby between San Fran, Palm Desert, and San Diego. Once my training was over, I moved off-base to a little bungalow Sierra found up in Mission Beach. It was pricey, but pretty nice digs for a sailor from Scaife, Pennsylvania. We settled into a routine life with daddy commuting down to Coronado every day like a regular businessman. A deployment would pop up, and I'd sail off, or hop in a jet and get back home like nothing ever happened. I couldn't ever tell Sierra where I was off to, or for how long, and that was good, because I wouldn't have wanted to, anyway."

"So, Buck was okay?"

"Buck was great. Sierra and Asia were great. We were very happy. Buck and I did five miles on the beach every morning before five a.m. and I hit the base before six. We had a blast. Sierra's parents both came to visit often, never together, of course. We had friends, and nice neighbors. I wish it didn't have to end."

"Why did it end?"

"I lost my job."

"What?"

"I was mustered out, got a purple heart, a disability check, and a pension. They sent me home for good."

"What happened?"

"I got hit in Grenada, and the Navy was done with me. It wasn't so bad, worked out well, actually, but I still miss that little place in Mission Beach."

"Okay, give me the details."

"I guess Asia was probably in fourth grade—just started, I think. I remember it was October. We were married, by the way, did that right after I finished SEAL qualifications back in '78. I got married in my dress whites on the beach in front of the Hotel Del Coronado. Sierra's mother arranged everything, and her father paid for it all. He liked me by then. But in '83 Reagan sent us to Grenada as part of Operation Urgent Fury, and I got hurt."

"Details."

"Buck was starting to get older, slowing down a lot. We weren't doing our morning run anymore, but we walked together every day. He was still my ninety pound alarm clock. I'd received a couple of promotions and a few commendations, so I went to the Caribbean as a Team leader. I was officially an E-4 when I got my discharge papers. We dropped into the drink and swam two miles into shore in the middle of the night. We were advance recon for the Marines. I got SEAL Team 6 organized in the surf. Our mission was to clear the beach of resistance and scout the route to the radio tower. The island only had one radio tower, and the Marines were tasked to capture it immediately. There were two machine gun nests on the beach. They were well placed with excellent lines of fire. That would have been the work of the Russians, but the Cubans that were manning them were clowns. I could smell them and see the glow of their cigars from in the water. They were sitting on the beach bunched together between their gun emplacements, smoking and passing a bottle of rum. It was easy. My Team stayed in the drink while I flanked them and slit their throats. I hope that doesn't make you squeamish."

"You ended up doing a lot of that."

"Yeah, I did, but those four were my first kills."

"Any regrets?"

"None, I'm an American sailor and a trained SEAL. Killing was my specialty, and I took it seriously. I believed we were the good guys, and I believed that we were right. I still do."

"I know."

"Besides, they were in uniform. That's important. I ended up fighting a lot of people that didn't wear uniforms or play by any of the rules. I was a little confused as a kid, but that all changed. I wasn't sure that McNamara and Kissinger knew what they were talking about with that whole domino theory thing, but when Vietnam fell in '75, and Cambodia, Laos, Thailand, and Burma followed . . . well, I knew there was good and there was bad. I figured we were good. I think guys like Haig, Ashcroft, and Rumsfeld are patriots, and I really don't give a damn what the French think about us. Liberty and democracy are not popularity contests. I've seen bad, and what liberal Americans consider brutal torture at Guantanamo strikes me as paddy-cake at a fraternity initiation. I know you don't think these are exactly Christian ideals . . ."

"You'd be surprised what I think."

"Okay, so anyway, we took the beach."

"Grenada?"

"Yeah, we took the beach in Grenada and advanced through the mangroves to the coast road. I set up a defensive line, and we waited for the Marines to land. There was a resort hotel right up the road from our position. I think it was a Ramada. The Grenadian soldiers and the Cubans were trashing the place. They were loading furniture into trucks, eating everything in the kitchen, and drinking the bar dry. We engaged them, killed a couple and captured the rest, and moved on toward the transmission tower. We took it without a fight, and my SEAL Team returned to our rendezvous point for pick-up. That's when the grenade blew up and I got my purple heart."

"That's when you lost your finger?"

"Just the tip of it, and it was my left hand, so it was no big deal. I learned quickly that nobody really needs the end of their baby finger. I adapted to picking my nose with my right hand, which was my dominant hand anyway."

"Got it."

"No pun intended, right? I'm sorry, but losing my hearing was much more of a handicap. The concussion blew out both of my eardrums and I lost seventy percent of my hearing, or so they said. I got hearing aids at Walter Reed about a year later, and it was as though nothing had changed. Going with limited auditory senses for a year was another one of those experiences that I'm glad I had. My other senses—the eyes especially—totally took over. I've always had great instincts and anticipation, and the ear problem really heightened my awareness of things. It's been like that my whole life. I had a crappy baseball glove, but it taught me to catch a ball with both hands. It improved my skills. I had a lousy bicycle, and I had to work hard to buy a second-hand car, but I learned how to work on those things, fix them, and appreciate them. I never had good skis. I always ended up with somebody else's hand-me-downs, but when I got out west, bought my first pair of new, shaped skis, and discovered soft, fluffy snow, those bitter cold, icy eastern winters had made me into a talented skier. I don't mean to sound corny or too much like a Pollyanna, but it turned out to be a blessing all around."

"Losing your hearing was a blessing?"

"Technically, my tympanic membranes both burst, and yes, it was definitely a blessing. I got sent home, got a better job with more money, and got to spend more time with my little family. I was ready to get out after almost nine years anyway, and this way was the golden ticket. I felt sorry for myself for about a week—missed the Team, the action, the command, the adrenaline, but I quickly realized how fast Asia was growing. I mean, I'd been around a lot, but never during the day. I didn't know anything about her school, her friends, or her budding love of ponies and horses. I suddenly had the day with Sierra, and that was great."

"What about the finger?"

"Like I said before, I didn't really need it. After awhile I didn't even notice it. I once saw a little boy on a dusty corner in Algiers. He was selling apples and baby snakes under a brightly painted sign that he must have made. I don't know what it said, but I assumed it said apples and baby snakes for sale. Don't ask me what the connection was, but this kid had the happiest grin on his face, and he had no legs. That made me reconsider what a minor inconvenience it was to lose a finger. A little girl in Zagora was staring at a bunch of fat U.N. soldiers when Graff and I drove by in a jeep one day. She was emaciated, and they were fat. They were drinking wine and acting stupid and this little kid was just staring at them. It occurred to me that when you're starving you have a different perspective. This girl wasn't going to ever have to worry about being obese or becoming an alcoholic. She was trying to survive day by day. The kid that tossed the grenade took the rebound in the face and died instantly, and that bothered me for a long time. I don't know why he was any different than the others, except that he was young. The boy I killed in Panama was the same story: too young to die, too young to be mixed up in a man's game. I still think of both of them. I still think of the woman, too."

"You need to talk about all three of them. This boy threw a hand grenade . . ."

"It was a Russian piece of crap. It should have killed me and two or three other guys around me. We'd let our guards down. We were standing on the beach waiting for the LCM 6 when this kid stepped from behind the mangroves and whipped the grenade at us. I saw it happen, caught it in mid-air, and tossed it back at him, all in slow motion. Combat always unfolded like a newsreel for me. It exploded half way between us, blew out my ears, took the tip of my finger—the hand at my side, not my throwing hand—and killed the kid. Another guy took shrapnel in the leg, but he wasn't close enough for any hearing damage. I've spent years thinking about why I threw it back at the kid; just instinct I guess, but I could just as easily have thrown it into the ocean or up the beach, anywhere else but back at him."

"He was trying to kill you. You should have been commended for saving the lives of your fellow soldiers."

"Sailors."

"I'm sorry?"

"We're sailors, not soldiers, and since I was the senior SEAL on the beach I was responsible for the after-action report, and that didn't get done until I was stateside again. My second in command should have taken that initiative, but, well, that didn't happen."

"Ernie would have been proud."

"That's great. I'm so blown away that you said that, because that's what I thought, too. I reacted without thinking and made the play. I did save lives, but I know I'll never forget that kid's face."

"You've shouldered a lifetime of guilt like it was a backpack permanently strapped to you."

"You betcha; guilt was a dish served hot at our dinner table. Some nights it was the only thing served hot. I was always guilty about something, and I rarely knew what it was. I think it was other people's expectations again. I just never felt like I was good enough. That's the thing that really worried me about flight training. I knew there was a lot of math involved in flying an aircraft, and that was something I had always struggled with. The old man always put me down about the algebra thing. Why wasn't I as smart as my sister or my brother? I ended up resenting them for that, but subconsciously I knew it wasn't their fault, so I felt guilty. It was a vicious circle, and it took me a long time to sort it out."

"Killing someone isn't as complicated though, is it?"

"No, if you feel guilty about ending somebody's life, it's pretty legitimate guilt. War is tough, and when there aren't clear rules of engagement, or it's not real evident who the enemy is, it gets tougher. Other than Grenada, I didn't fight in any traditional wars where the other guys wore uniforms and flew flags. That made it harder."

"How did you keep getting mixed up in armed conflicts if you were out of the Navy?"

"I was evac'ed to some hick hospital in Louisiana, didn't stay long, just overnight, but when I was waiting for transport back to my base some guy came up to me in the dayroom and handed me his card. I never looked at it until I was home for about a week, but when I found out what the score was I knew I had to find work, and I dug it out of my sea bag. I was scared. I had a pretty good idea what it was like to be a husband and a father, but that was when I had a job. Now, all of a sudden the whole responsibility gig hit me. How was I going to provide for this little family? I mean I had some options: disability pay, accrued leave pay, insurance, Sierra's family, but they didn't seem like long-term answers. I found the guy's card and called him."

"Who was this guy?"

"I don't remember his name. He was a recruiter for FoxBlade, and he said he'd fly out the next day to talk with me. He did, too. Showed up at our door about noon and surprised the heck out of me. I don't know what I was expecting, but the next hour changed my life forever."

"What happened? And what is FoxBlade?"

"FoxBlade Mining and Marine Enterprises was the name of the company he represented, the name of the company I ended up working for most of the rest of my life. They changed it to FoxBlade Logistical Services Company somewhere down the road. The guy arrived with bagels, believe it or not. He was real nice to Asia, come to think of it. She must have been out of school, so it was probably Saturday or maybe even Sunday. I don't remember, but Sierra liked him too, and when he offered me the job we were both floored."

"Why? What job? Why were you floored?"

"The job was pretty sketchy. I don't remember exactly how he explained it. He said that they were an international firm specializing in mining and drilling operations all over the world. They had security concerns, and provided goods and material and services for other big companies outside of America. He said they were interested in people with my experience, which meant command and control, and then he offered me a lot of money."

"What kind of money?"

"Don't laugh, remember this was 1983. He said he was prepared to tender a starting salary of $100,000 a year with a cash bonus of $50,000 to cover moving and other expenses."

"Yikes, what did you say?"

"I said, yes, you moron. Oh, excuse me."

"You're excused, and then what happened?"

"He left a contract for me to look over, and Sierra, Asia, and I ran it out to Palm Springs to ask her father what he thought. He took one look at it and asked me who they wanted me to kill. He didn't know how prophetic that question was."

"Then what happened?"

"I called Joe up, that was his name, Joe Lloyd. I called him and said that I had signed the contract and he sent me three tickets to Dallas. Two days later we were in FoxBlade's executive dining room having lunch with the founder and CEO of the company. I didn't see a lot of old Joe after that. We got the grand tour, got introduced to a very nice realtor that Sierra spent the next three weekends with, and I went to work. It was all logistical stuff early on, but I caught on quickly, and pretty soon I was flying around the world making sure that all the crazy things we were doing for Alcoa, IBM, Siemens, Pfizer, Anaconda, Texaco, and all the rest of our customers were getting done. Sierra found us a nice little ranch over in Euless, and when Asia got out of school we all moved in. Euless wasn't as grown up then as it is now, but it was still tough for the girls. Dallas isn't southern California."

"But eventually you ended up back in California, right?"

"Well, yeah, but not for a long time. There were a couple of moves and a lot of life in between."

"Okay, so what happened in Dallas?"

"Things were going well in Texas, actually; at least we were both trying hard to make it work. I had my job, and I approached it like everything else, full tilt. It was my new duty, so to speak. I threw myself into my work, but realized within a couple of months that I was spending more time than I wanted to away from Sierra and Asia. My bride was working at making the adjustment. She'd put Asia in a new school that we were happy with, and they were both making friends, but, I don't know, they weren't so much really friends as polite acquaintances. We didn't seem to be forging any tight bonds. There was a cultural difference, I mean, these were Texans. I was a responsible, dependable employee, but I began to feel a dereliction to my real duty—to Sierra and Asia."

"Duty's important to you."

"It is, and we were both dancing around the truth, afraid of expressing our real feelings. I thought that she was happy, and she thought I was happy, and neither one of us wanted to get in the way of each other's happiness."

"You probably felt selfish. You've always been too sensitive about the feelings of people you love. If you misread their feelings, you run the risk of hurting them. You needed to keep things simple, that's a reoccurring thing with you. You know instinctively to do the right thing, but then you over think it."

"You're right, of course, and that's exactly what was happening in Dallas. Asia didn't know the difference, but Sierra and I were both faking it. Neither one of us could wait to go, so when the time came we were like two birds jumping off a wire together."

"What happened?"

"FoxBlade started picking up these government contracts. The State Department was doing all kinds of crazy stuff in foreign countries, and they needed some people with experience to get them in the right places with the right people. We knew all about ports, factories, refineries, mining operations, transportation systems, and stuff like food distribution routes; it was the kind of thing we specialized in for private companies, so we got the work. This was all starting to come down right after the attack on our Marine barracks in Beirut, so the writing was pretty much on the wall. I was in on everything from the very beginning. It was my military experience of course, but I'd done a good job before we started getting all of this government work, so . . ."

"What about leaving Dallas?"

"I'm getting to that, sheesh. Okay, so all this new stuff required a closer relationship with the people that eventually became our biggest customer."

"The State Department?"

"The CIA actually."

"Really, the spooks?"

"Nice, but yeah, the spooks. The work appealed to my sense of patriotism, by the way."

"Duty again."

"Sure, I was the go-to guy. They sent me to D.C. to set up a satellite office outside of Columbia, Maryland. I made a whole lot more money, and I recruited a whole new staff of freedom fighting ass-kickers. The work was lucrative. We were the pros; we knew the harbor masters, knew who ran the process plants, the oil refineries, the sewage treatment facilities. We knew who made the trains run, and though I didn't anticipate ever being in the line of fire again, I certainly had the experience to run covert and clandestine operations in Indian country."

"So you left Texas?"

"Yeah, Dallas and Fort Worth were really growing. Euless was out by the airport, and it was expanding like crazy. We leased our little ranch to a supervisor for a construction outfit working on the airport for twice as much as our monthly mortgage, and things looked pretty good. We found a great piece of property on the bay within commuting distance of the Capital, and built our dream house. Sierra found a good school for Asia, and she finished up fourth grade and eventually graduated from St. Anne's in Annapolis and then boarded at Timothy through high school. I say eventually because we lived in Italy while she was in fifth grade, but we came back and she matriculated with her eighth grade class. Saint Timothy's has a nice little equestrian thing going, so after the pony, we bought her a horse, you know the drill. Everything was working out fine, except I hated having Asia away at boarding school, but it was close by, and that's what she wanted. The move and the change in responsibilities gave me the opportunity to spend more time with my wife and my daughter; Asia was home on the weekends, so it was cool. I still traveled, but not as much, and I wasn't ever low man on the totem pole again. I sent all of our guys through advanced training; the Agency helped smooth the way for that, and of course, I participated too, but I wasn't ever away from home for very long at a time."

"What kind of training?"

"You know, your questions are starting to get kind of predictable."

"That's good, then I won't have to ask as many."

"We did desert survival training with the Marines at Yuma MCAS about twenty miles north of the Mexican border. We drilled in the sand and the heat with the guys from Fighter Training Squadron 401, part of Marine Aircraft group 13. We did weapons training at Fort Bliss in El Paso where we had instructors from the Army Sergeants-Major Academy. We took cold weather and mountain training from the people at Mountain Home Air Force base outside of Twins Falls, Idaho. I sent the guys to Fort Campbell in Kentucky for languages. Austin Peay State University actually has a satellite campus on the base. Then we went to Fort Irwin, California, where the Tenth Mountain Division has mock desert villages set up. The teams learned GPS and computer control recon and communication tactics there."

"Wow."

"Yeah, FoxFire didn't spare any expense, but we mostly paid our own way, nothing was on the American taxpayer."

"I thought the company was FoxBlade."

"Well, yeah, until we moved to Columbia. I think Dallas wanted a little distance built into the arrangement. I never liked either name, but they both looked fine on the paycheck."

"It sounds like you were happy to get back to the East Coast."

"I was—we were—but I wasn't unhappy in Texas. I'm sorry, that's a lie. I felt obliged to FoxBlade for the career move, and I was committed to see things through there, but it wasn't just all about me anymore. I realize now that I was ready to bolt, and I probably would have if I'd known how unhappy Sierra was, but I held on. I did my job, tried to take it day by day, and things worked out. It's funny how providence and patience work. I prayed for a change, but I tended to my knitting and let things unravel at their own pace. I examined my dreams and my intentions and tried to communicate and express that in my daily meditative reflections, and then I let it go, and whammo."

"Whammo like you got what you wanted?"

"Whammo like I got what I needed. I've always been careful to not ask for stuff for me. I pray for the safety and security of my family. I ask for peace and harmony for Sierra and Asia. I just want them to be happy, content, and hopeful, but I'm not in the results business. I do the asking and leave the rest to God."

"That sounds like a good policy."

"It's easy when things are working out okay. When Asia got hurt it wasn't so easy. I was tested."

"When was that?"

"Later, I had some bad times when the despair and the fear came around. When my baby got hurt, when the nightmares about the killing started, when Buck passed, Penelope too, and my parents died, and Sierra's mother got sick."

"Who is Penelope?"

"She was Asia's pony. She coliced and died. That was tough. All of that was tough. I was kind of looking around wondering what I'd done wrong."

"What'd you come up with?"

"The dead kid on the beach at Grenada. I figured it was karma, payback. I was mad because I thought I was living right, but . . . ."

"You felt let down?"

"I felt deceived. No, betrayed, I felt betrayed."

DECEPTION AND DISILLUSSION

"Who deceived you?"

"Who do you think? No, that's not fair, I'm sorry. I've done a lot of deceiving myself. The next couple of years, heck longer than that, but the next set of years, anyhow, was all about deception. It was all smoke and mirrors. I lived an undercover operation in a foreign country for over fifteen months, and it was all a lie. The worst part of it was that I dragged my wife and daughter into it, too."

"Tell me what happened."

"We needed intel in the Middle East. Lebanon was too hot, Syria was full of bad guys, Israel was an ally, Saudi, Egypt, and the Emirates were crawling with American and European businessmen, so I set up a storefront in Italy. We needed a way to gather intelligence on what was going on around the Med, and southern Italy seemed like a pretty good place to do it. Socialism was on the rise, crazy Muslims were running around everywhere, the Red Brigade was in its glory, and anti-Americanism was rampant. Italy was close enough to the action but far enough to be relatively safe. Asia was about ten by then, maybe eleven, and I needed a place where I felt confident that none of us was going to end up kidnapped or something."

"So you opened a store?"

"That's just a figure of speech. I spent some time researching the situation and decided that we should set up a business that would let us interact with some of the players—terrorists, threats, targets, and big money boys."

"What kind of business?"

"The oil business, of course. The embassy in Lebanon had been attacked in '82, the Marine barracks a year later, and we were clueless. The one business that seemed to open all the doors to every facet of every culture was fuel and lubrication. I decided to set up a lube oil venture because it was good cover and good bait. I was also a little afraid of gas tanks blowing up, so we stayed away from fuels. We had lots of friends in the business, and I recruited a couple of civilian types that knew the nuts and bolts. None of them ever suspected that they were working undercover for the American government much less as bait for bad guys. I had to play a convincing part as the moneyed capital venture guy, so we moved to the continent for a year, a little more as it turned out."

"And stated drilling for oil?"

"No, our business was way down the process chain from drilling operations. We blended various grades and types of lubricants like motor oils, hydraulic oils, marine lubricants, that kind of thing. We brought in highly refined base oils in large quantities, so we needed a waterfront facility with a deep-water pier to off-load big tankers. The Navy researched that for us. We needed large holding tanks for the base stocks and liquid additives. We had to have blending equipment and facilities, and smaller finished product tanks, and the Army Corps of Engineers helped us with that. We needed rail access and truck loading and receiving racks, as well as warehouse, lab, and office space, and our new employees with the experience of years at Shell, BP, Total Fina, and Exxon designed that stuff. It was nine months before we shipped our first tank truck of motor oil and another year before we were up and running our packaging lines, but the time was well spent."

"You had packaging lines?"

"Sure, we filled pints, liters, and gallons of multi-grade lubes. We had high speed filling equipment. This was great stuff; I was having a ball. Asia was the perfect age to travel, so we spent weekends driving all over Italy. We took holidays in the Alps and the French Riviera, and, of course, we had to go to Israel, Egypt, you know. My boys were gathering all kinds of information on creepy people that didn't like our country. One of my ex-SEALS was even sleeping with a Corsican girl who was a member of the Red Brigade. The intelligence we were sending back to Washington was gold. The Achille Lauro was hijacked in October 1985, and we were able to get three of our guys on board when she sailed back into Syrian waters. Our team identified the four PLO bad guys and followed them off the ship at Port Said after they'd cut a deal. They boarded an Egyptian airliner to fly them back to Tunisia and our guys followed them on board and radioed co-ordinates to the F-14's off the

USS Saratoga that intercepted the flight and forced it to land at the UN base in Sigonella. I personally gave my men permission to take down the leader, Abu Abbas, but the Italians protected him. He got his shortly after we caught up with him again in Iraq in 2003. That was the kind of good work our little deception enabled."

"How did you fool everybody?"

"We didn't fool anybody. We were a legitimate business operation. Sure, we had deep pockets provided by the CIA and State Department, and the truth is, we all got a little rich. We built a company overnight with OPM, and we were getting paychecks from FoxBlade and FoxFire and our own little company, Alsierra Lubricantes.

"OPM?"

"Other people's money and Alsierra is, of course, Asia Sierra Lubes."

"Of course. Where exactly was the factory?"

"Taranto. It was perfect, located in the instep of the Italian boot with direct access to the Med and the Aegean Sea. Asia went to fifth grade at an American school there, a little heavy on the religion, but that didn't hurt. I was worried about the curriculum and her progress, but when she got back to St. Anne's she hadn't missed a beat."

"What was the deception?"

"That's obvious, we were spooks, but there were other things, too, personal things. I had to have backgrounds on all my people and all potential targets, so I ended up knowing more about folks than I wanted to, especially me. Women were a problem. There was one particular time with a woman that came real close to deception of the marital fidelity suit. I was leading a double life, and it wasn't natural to me. I couldn't distinguish between the James Bond character, the big-shot businessman, the retired SEAL, the devoted father and husband, or the scared kid from Frazier, Pennsylvania. Sometimes I felt like I was standing on the threshold of insanity banging on the door."

"How long was it before you realized that you were already inside that door?"

"That's very funny, but I guess you know it's also very true. I was totally overwhelmed at that point in my life. The more information I acquired on our adversaries, the more frightened I became for myself and my family. There were a number of local incidents leading up to the Achille Lauro thing that freaked me out. In October of 1983 one of our senior Navy officers was assassinated by the November 17 group in Athens. In March of '84 Bill Buckley was kidnapped and murdered in Beirut by the Islamic Jihad. I knew both of those guys. A month after Buckley's death, eighteen servicemen were killed in a restaurant bombing outside an Air Force base in Spain, and then in June 1985, the TWA Rome to Athens flight was hijacked by Hezbollah terrorists. The crew and passengers were held for seventeen days in Algiers and Beirut. These were very real threats, and I kept thinking that something like that might happen to Asia, Sierra, or me. The Achille Lauro hijacking came four months later, and I was totally paranoid."

"So you were disillusioned?"

"Yeah, I said paranoid, but, yeah, I hadn't thought the danger through, and to be quite honest, I started questioning our motives, my country's motives. Maybe we were wrong about a lot of stuff. There sure seemed to be a bunch of people hating us."

"That hasn't seemed to change much. How were women a problem?"

"They weren't, not normally anyway. There was one woman in Casablanca, though, that presented a problem. I had to fly over to Morocco to meet with Graff. He was CIA. I landed in Rabat and he met me at the airport. He handed me a Glock when we got out to his car. We couldn't carry weapons when we were traveling, of course. I'd trained with a Beretta M9 in the Navy and qualified with the Beretta 92FS, but I liked this Glock. It was the G19, and it made me feel like I was back in action. I'm not sure why I mention it, except thinking back on it years later, I always figured that as soon as I grabbed that gun that afternoon trouble started following me. We drove south along the coast and stopped for a late lunch in a nice little café looking out over the ocean. I think it was Mohammedia. We watched the sun set into the Atlantic as I watched Graff begin to get very drunk. He had been sent from Washington a couple of weeks earlier to brief me, and he had intel on all our people and a lot of the people and organizations that we were supposed to be watching, spying on actually. He also had a little tidbit of info on me that I hadn't been aware of, and it shocked my world."

"Is this leading to the problem with women?"

"It is, but the background info that Graff had on me is a lot more important."

"How's that?"

"He told me that my father wasn't really my father."

"That'll do it. When it comes to delusion, deception, and resentment the old 'he's not really your father' trick works every time."

"Do you think this is funny?"

"Of course not, but somehow I think you've dealt with it. You were probably suspicious about it for a very long time."

"That's not true. You're right, I've dealt with it, and when I look at the situation objectively, I even understand it a little, but I had no inclination about it before Graff got piss drunk and blurted it out. I was shocked."

"What did you do?"

"I almost killed him. I told him he was full of it, I thought he'd made it up. I was in denial, freaked out. I insisted he explain himself, prove it, I don't know. I really don't remember what I said or did. I was driving at that point, because he was smashed and I wasn't sure if he was being straight with me or not. I had my hand on the Glock, I remember that."

"Did you want to kill him?"

"I think I did. I wasn't being rational, but I believed him and I thought that if I killed him nobody else would find out."

"Find out what?"

"Find out that my mother was sleeping with my father's brother while he had been overseas."

"So it was your uncle?"

"Technically, it was my dad."

"Yeah, I guess it was. Did your father know?"

"I never asked him, but I don't think so. How the CIA found out, I'll never know, but I do know it's true. It all adds up."

"Maybe that's why your father ran around. So tell me about your issue with women."

"That incident happened the same day, believe it or not. It was only the one time. I mean I'd been tempted before, but I really was head over heels in love with Sierra."

"Go on."

"We got to Casablanca; Graff had driven up from Marrakech the day before. We checked into the Hyatt Regency as American businessmen. I was the owner of Alsierra Lubes and he was a supplier. I don't remember the details, but he passed out as soon as we got to my room, and I went back downstairs."

"You were drinking?"

"I wasn't, not really, not much anyway. I've never really been much of a drinker, but this guy had a hollow leg. He never even seemed to get drunk, but then boom, he was out. Morocco is a Muslim country, and they frown on alcohol. They know American businessmen are going to use it though, so it's available. Moving on, Graff passes out, I go down to the restaurant and have dinner. I still remember it: coconut cakes, mint tea, almond milk, melon with more mint, more almonds in the eggplant salad, couscous with red peppers, coriander, cumin, and saffron, and lamb kebabs for the entrée. I washed with warm scented water between each course, and then went to the bar for a glass of raki. That's where I met her."

"Sounds delicious."

"It was, she was too, I'm sure, but luckily I never found out. The food in Italy was spectacular, of course, but nothing like Morocco. That's another disappointment come to think of it. Why does American food all taste the same?"

"The girl."

"She was Ethiopian. She'd been sitting at the bar alone for about an hour, so I sat beside her. There was some flirtation going on. I noticed her watching me about half-way through the couscous. She was stunning. I don't remember her name because I knew it was a lie as soon as I heard it. I thought she was a hooker, especially when I saw the tattoo, but she wasn't. She was a spy, and she was on to me."

"Tell me about the tattoo."

"It was adorable. I don't recall her name, but I'll never forget that tattoo. It struck me as a little inappropriate for such an exotic woman. It was playful, cute, and unpretentious. She had the most beautiful skin color and very toned arms, and right on her muscley little bicep was the most delightful and mischievous rendition of Betty Boop. She had her back turned, and her head was turned around with a come-hither grin on her face, and her little skirt was lifted high on her thighs, and she had the most perfect Afro hairdo you ever saw. I was totally enamored. Bells were ringing in my head. I knew this dame meant business, but something wasn't right. It was just too easy. I had a room on the tenth floor of the Hyatt with a stunning view of the harbor and the old city, but when we walked into the room she marched right over to Graff passed out on the couch and felt his pulse."

"She felt his pulse?"

"He was the one she had been tailing for a week, and apparently when he picked me up at the airport, my cover was blown. When he didn't come out of the room that evening she turned her attention to me hoping to find him. Feeling his pulse tipped her hand. My instincts were too sharp not to notice that this was strange behavior. She realized she'd screwed up, and went for her bag. That's when Graff shot her in the back."

"How brutal, what did you do?"

"I couldn't believe it. I was shocked. We needed to get rid of her body, of course. There was very little blood, thank God. Sorry. I realized that Graff was still drunk, but he was all business; said she'd been following him since he'd arrived and that she was a KGB operative. He said that she was going to kill us both."

"Did you believe that?"

"I didn't know what to believe. I do know there wasn't a gun in her bag, but I never mentioned that to Graff. I was in a panic. We decided to walk her through the lobby in the middle of the night and get her into the car so we could dump her in the desert. Graff showed me her picture and her CIA profile while we waited for the wee hours. He showed me all the other enemy operatives in the area that he had info on, and then he showed me the detailed background on all of our people too; including me. He had a dossier on me that included incredible detail of my whole life, and of course, my life before I was born."

"That included your mother's relationship with your uncle, I presume."

"Yeah, it did."

"That must have hurt."

"Well, the whole night was like a macabre dream. I felt so terrible about the dead woman, but I felt guilty too, that I had brought her up to the room with the intention of cheating on my wife. We walked her through the hotel right before dawn and headed east out into the desert. I felt so ashamed of myself. It seemed to me then that morals were the sole prerogative of good people like Sierra."

"We're all sinners."

"I was a murderer and an adulterer, and I hated myself. We drove toward Fes and buried her in the sand before we got to the Algerian border. We made contact with Graff's local at El Gor, and he gave us the information Graff was supposed to get on the Al Quaeda training camp at Ras Elma. We drove into the Yakouren forest in Tizi Ouzou Province and photographed the camp."

"So we're back to Thucydides?"

"Huh?"

"Or was it Thrasymachus who said, 'Might makes right'?"

"Whoever, I don't know, but you're right. I was struggling with that big brother/policeman of the world thing. It didn't help that we'd just killed a woman, and suddenly I found myself trying to come to grips with what exactly my mission was. That was also the day I saw the starving little girl in Zagora. It was all part of the delusion I was feeling."

"What did you do?"

"We got back to Rabat. I got on a plane for Rome, drove home to Taranto, hugged Sierra, and told her we were going home. I'd had enough of Europe and the whole charade. I would have loved to run that business legitimately in America, or somewhere else. Australia or New Zealand might have been cool, but it wasn't meant to be. I kept my cover though, and returned to Taranto a number of times over the next two years to check on the plant and do the CIA's dirty little jobs."

"You kept returning to Italy?"

"Sure, that's why I was there when the Achille Lauro hijacking went down."

"So you basically stayed in the same line of work?"

"Oh, yeah, but I was even more active than before. I became an advisor and went into the Persian Gulf in 1988 with SEAL Teams 1 and 2. Army Intel had identified the mines that sank the USS Sam Roberts, and Operation Prime Chance was our revenge mission. The next year was Panama and that was ugly."

"Uglier than the other missions?"

"Panama was where I killed the other young boy and the woman. It haunts me. I should have been out of the game by then, but I'd become a pro, a mercenary. That's where I was captured and tortured too, but I got sprung and took care of the creeps that entertained themselves at my expense."

"Okay, tell me about Panama."

"It was December of '89. Asia had just come out of the coma. That was a relief. I hated to leave her, but it was as though I had to take my fear out on something, so I went. The code name was Operation Just Cause. I was with SEAL Teams 2 and 4 in Task Unit Papa. Our mission was to seize Paitilla Airfield and blow up Noriega's plane so he couldn't escape. We did that okay, but the woman was one of a half dozen enemy combatants that engaged us. She came around the side of a hangar with a big ass SAM, and I let her have it. She was tiny. I remember thinking how strange it was for her to be carrying such an unwieldy weapon for such a small person. Who knows what that SAM would have tracked down and destroyed if she'd managed to fire it?"

"Asia was probably in college I guess."

"What? No, I mean, well, no, like sixteen or something. She was still at the Timothy School. I'm talking about killing somebody."

"I want to know about Asia. That's really what's bothering you now. How'd your little girl get hurt?"

"It was at the Devon Horse Show up in Pennsylvania. She got tossed. I was out of the country and didn't find out until the next day. I rushed home and found her in the hospital. Sierra said the doctors weren't sure if she would ever regain consciousness, or if there would be brain damage if she did. It was terrible. I felt terrible."

"More shame?"

"Of course, I was ashamed. I'd been off playing GI Joe again, defending my country from shadows and threats, and my baby was almost killed. I blamed Sierra. I blamed the trainer, and I blamed myself. We were living in the nicest little place, and I was never there. I had two wonderful girls in my life, and I basically ignored them. I was so selfish, but I thought that it was selfless of me to work so hard and bring home the bacon so that they could have . . . I dunno, stuff. My priorities were pretty messed up."

"Sounds like it."

"Unfortunately, they stayed that way for a good while longer."

"What about Buck?"

"What about him? I was trying to tell you about the woman and the kid I felt so bad about killing. How'd we get on Buck and Asia?"

"I want to hear about the things you felt deceived about, deluded about, and disappointed about. Your mother, too. What was your despair all about?"

"Yeah, I get that, but you're kinda interrupting my flow here."

"Too bad, what happened to Asia; then tell me about Buck?"

"Asia came through it okay, but we were scared, real scared. I prayed and prayed and began to doubt."

"What did you doubt?"

"I doubted you."

"Not me, buster, never mind, we'll get to that. When did Buck die?"

"That was earlier. He passed before we went to Italy. One of the reasons I wouldn't sell the house was that Buck was buried in the back yard. Hey, old dogs die. It broke my heart, but we all have our time. My mother's time came, and not long after the old man died, too. I copped a real resentment over my sister's drama when they died."

"In what way?"

"Her extortionate, melodramatic grief, that's what way. My sister has always been the tragedy queen, the martyr, bemoaning her self-sacrifice and wearing it like a bloody tourniquet. Asia spent thirty-three days in a coma at Johns Hopkins and she never visited once."

"Why not?"

"I presume because Asia didn't have any money to leave to her."

"Ouch."

"I don't care; it's true. I mean I know I had been selfish, but in a way, I thought my motives were pretty pure. It's childish I know, but all children are selfish, and all children believe they are right. I thought that I was always on the side of right; providing for my family, defending my country, you know."

"We're back to 'might makes right'?"

"In a way, both sides in any conflict believe that they are right, that they have the ethical and moral high ground. The problem is that when both parties believe they are right, who wins? You have to interject a third opinion, the referee that decides, the tertium quid, so to speak."

"That's good, I like that."

"Yeah, the tertium quid is ultimately God, but once again, both guys think that God is on their side, so it comes down to firepower—might makes right whether it's really right or not. So I don't forgive myself for killing a boy in Grenada or shooting a woman in Panama. I don't care about the others I killed; they were soldiers, they were combatants."

"These two were combatants too, though, and what about the other boy?"

"Look, it may be a skewed code, but it's my skewed code. The other kid was my jailer. After we took the airfield, we set up a defensive perimeter that was overrun. I was captured. They executed the guys in uniform, but they took me prisoner because they thought I was a spy. They were right. I was a spy. They chained me to a wall in an office at the airfield and did disgusting things to me until I passed out. They weren't even trying to question me about anything. The kid was sent in to mop up my vomit and piss, and I snapped his neck with my feet. He thought I was still unconscious and he got a little too close. I used his teeth to saw through the rope around my wrists and then I slipped out the window. I killed a soldier, took his weapon, and killed everyone in the building. I saw the kid's mangled jawbone in my sleep for a couple of years. Sometimes I feel sorry for myself, think that I've suffered with my nightmares, but then I realize that at least I'm alive. I'm still dreaming, right? It's easy to use your grief as a crutch, or in Asia's case, as a weapon, but you have to move on."

"What about your parents and your sister?"

"I really don't think of them very much. It's all about Sierra, Asia, and Buck; always was, always will be. My sister's still around, of course, and I miss Mom sometimes, but . . . hey, let me tell you a cool thing about the old doll. First off, you have to recognize that she had a tough life. It was hard to live with him, especially I guess, with the big secret they were both keeping from the world. There was definitely a lot of disappointment in her life, but I have one precious memory. We were at the grocery store together when JFK was murdered. People were wailing in the aisles and hugging each other in the parking lot, and my mom was real upset, too. Mom and I were never alone together, but for some reason we were that day. I might have stayed home from school—faking it probably. The next morning, though, while the whole country was mourning in shock, mom discovered that C.S. Lewis had died the day before as well. Lewis and Kennedy both died on the same day, and my mother sat me down and explained the difference in the two men. She thought that the loss of C.S. Lewis was much more significant than the loss of the President. It was something we shared."

"I love it, that's a great story. So, there was intimacy with your mother?'

"Sure, I loved my mother. We had our special moments. As I grew older, I took it upon myself to try to defend her from his rampages. That never went well. I guess I was ultimately disappointed in her that she didn't leave him, but I have a different perspective now. Dad was just incapable of displaying affection. He was also incapable of processing any emotional honesty. Times were different; she was doing what she thought was right, what she thought she needed to do."

"Okay, what's left, Sierra's mother?"

"Well, that turned into a pretty sad situation, too, but there wasn't any deceit or delusion involved, just more disappointment, I guess. We had moved back to California by then. Asia was in her first year at UCSB, and we'd bought our dream house in the mountains above Santa Barbara. Leaving Maryland wasn't hard except for the house on the bay. Sierra had really turned that waterfront property into something special. I think she had a little bit of Shushu in her. I almost dug Buck up and brought his bones along with us. The Chesapeake was cool, too; I mean living on the water. We'd gotten used to East Coast living—well, maybe not the winters. Winter on Chesapeake Bay can be pretty brutal, but Sierra had made that a very special home, and we all felt relaxed there. My wife was no modern day Lilly Barton. She came from money, but she wasn't at all ostentatious or superficial. Her decorating skills were wonderful, and she made every house we ever lived in comfortable and pleasant. By the time Asia was ready for college, though, I was pretty well set financially, and I could really call the shots. Jobs and deployments kept popping up, and I kept trying to price myself out of the business, but the Agency wouldn't let me just walk away. They liked my work, and to a certain extent, I think they had to protect me to protect some of their secrets. Sometimes I felt like I was holding on to a runaway horse; like I was Secretariat's jockey. It certainly made sense to keep me close, anyway."

"Sierra's mother?"

"There you go again. We're getting there, pal. Like I said, I kept demanding more money for overseas work, hoping that they'd realize that they could get a younger, cheaper guy, but it wasn't meant to be. I had done a lot of the follow up investigation work after the Lockerbie thing in '88 . . ."

"What Lockerbie thing?"

"Pan Am 103, remember? There was the World Trade Center bombing in 1993, and I went to Saudi Arabia using my old oil executive cover to help out after the Air Force housing bombs in 1996. Our embassies in Kenya and Tanzania were attacked in 1998, and I was sent there, but it wasn't until the USS Cole attack that Al Qaeda started hunting me."

"This is leading to Sierra's mother's situation?"

"Slowly, yeah, it is. The girls had been visiting her at least two or three times every year. She was holding up well, aging gracefully. She had a full life, but suddenly the Alzheimer's kicked in, and it was a good thing we were living on the West Coast again. After the Cole incident, I was sent to the Middle East a couple of times running down leads, and I hooked up with Graff again on my last trip there. I couldn't believe the guy was still alive, much less still in the game. He showed me a captured dossier the bad guys had on me, and I realized my secret spy days were over. We'd heard that Khalid Sheikh Mohammed had been spotted on the island of Djerba off the coast of Tunisia, so we went there looking for him. It was a trap."

"Who got trapped?"

"Me, it was my fault. I knew trouble was brewing. I'd always had an innate sense about that sort of thing. My intuition bell would always sound when darkness was approaching, when I felt menace creeping up behind me, but this time I shook it off. I purposely ignored my well tuned danger antennae, and I shut the eyes that were always open in the back of my head."

"What happened?"

"Like I said, I got sloppy. Thinking back on it, I realized that I should have known that I was starting to lose my edge. That damn Graff—I'll blame him. I'd always met trouble head on, but this time I went to Djerba not just to meet trouble, but to make it."

"And what happened?"

"I died."

DEATH AND DESPAIR

"What do you mean you died?"

"We were supposed to meet our informant inside the El Ghriba synagogue. This was about six months after 9/11. It was Graff's fault, poor devil; every time I got around that idiot bad things happened. A crazed terrorist drove a tanker filled with natural gas right up the front steps of the place and slammed it into the massive oak doors. We were standing about twenty feet from the thing. Nothing happened for a minute, and people just froze. I started running toward the back when the explosion caught me from behind and threw me the length of the temple. I woke up in a hospital bed beside a little boy. Twenty-one people were dead including Graff and this French kid's parents. We were among the thirty odd injured casualties, and then I found out that the boy's sister, Justine, had survived too. It was the perfect out for me. The Agency declared me dead and buried, and I was no longer on the terrorist wanted list. It took me a couple months to recover, and while I was healing I got to know Justine and her little brother, Oliver. When we were all ready to be released I pulled some strings and got them American passports and brought them both home to Santa Barbara."

"Did you ever get Khalid?"

"No, as far as I know he's still running around. This is where we tie into Sierra's mother, though. Our new place in the hills had a great little guest cottage, but it was actually too big and too far away from the main house to put Sierra's mother there. We all loved her very much and wanted to take care of her ourselves; at least as much as we could. It was tough, though, having her in the main house, and like I said the guest house wasn't safe for her to be in alone. Justine and Oliver solved our problem. Justine was probably about five or six years older than Asia; maybe twenty-five I think. Oliver was ten or eleven. We put them in the cottage with Sierra's mom, and I paid Justine a weekly salary to take care of the old girl. We all had our meals together whenever I was home, well, dinner at least, and it turned out to be a pretty good arrangement. Oliver went to school up in Mission Canyon, and he loved it. He picked up the language right away, and he was a real hit with the little girls. He was a tough little guy, and that was good since he'd lost his parents, plus his soccer skills and his French accent made him very popular. Justine was wonderful with Sierra's mom. She was still dealing with the sudden loss of her own parents and I think it helped her. I'll always remember the first time I saw her when she came into the men's ward in the hospital to visit her little brother. She had a tragic little round-face like a fully bloomed moon orchid. I knew Sierra would love her. Eventually, she wanted to take nursing courses, so we sent her into Santa Barbara to the hospital three nights a week, and that was perfect for Sierra who got to spend a couple of quiet evenings with her mother."

"How did this all work for you?"

"Things couldn't have been better. It felt like we had planted our own little Eden. There was a stable right down the canyon from us where Asia boarded her horse, and I started taking lessons and eventually bought a horse of my own. I hadn't really been too close to any of our animals since Buck died, but this guy filled that hole. He was part Arabian and part quarter horse, and he ended up being the perfect horse for me. Asia's new trainer had me try a dozen different mounts, but this horse and I really hit it off. I was never the country club type. I wasn't going to retire to the golf course or take up sailing or anything. Riding fit the need, and of course, I still skied. I hadn't done much skiing back East, but now that I was just a couple hours from real mountains I picked it up again. Life was good. Sierra's mom wasn't great, but she was comfortable and in good spirits. The dementia made her act childlike sometimes, but unlike some other older folks, she was delightful. Justine was very gentle with her. She sang to her in French. It was very sweet."

"It all sounds very idyllic."

"It was, until I got the call to go to Afghanistan."

"Why'd you go?"

"I went because of 9/11. Things were fine in Santa Barbara, but in a way that I realize now, I was kinda faking it. I was infuriated that three thousand Americans had been murdered, and I wanted revenge. I wanted to hunt down Osama bin Laden and slice him open myself. I had spent close to two months in a Corsican hospital bed thinking about that bastard, and I wanted to find him and kill him. That's probably why I went to Liberia, too. At the time I felt as though I was losing my spiritual connection, my moral compass seemed to be pointing in the wrong direction. I thought I had a hole in my heel and my goodness was leaking out. I still thought that I was right about everything, but I was tired, and I wasn't sure that my country was right about everything anymore. I'd done my share, but I felt unappreciated and, frankly, I wanted to kill some more."

"You were very angry, very confused."

"It was more than that though; the pain of my own belligerence and defiance was eating at me. I'd started drinking too much, and the whiskey had become an arrow in my side that I was walking around with. The day I arrived home with Oliver and Justine, I wanted to leave again, but I knew it was wrong, so I fought it. I stuffed it, but it came out sideways. The booze didn't help. I had happiness, but I just couldn't see it. I was incapable of clinging to the joy, unable to experience the moment. It seemed as though I was trying to squeeze good emotions out of a rotten lemon, and I was losing it. I was riding my horse—and trying to be happy—and basically watching my life fall through the cracks. I needed the action again."

"So . . . ?"

"So, I chased it. I figure there are basically three ways that I can address a problem: I can handle it myself, assert my will and make it go my way—I can ask for advice, which never works because then I have someone to blame if things don't work out—or I can simply surrender to it, tell the world that I can't handle it and ask for help. Asking for help is different than asking for advice."

"Okay, which did you do?"

"Neither. I tried to handle it myself, and that meant suiting up, getting on an airplane, and flying to Afghanistan to kill bad guys."

"Probably not the best choice."

"No, this time I really did die, but because they had faked my death before, I had this feeling of invincibility. I had the kryptonite in my pocket and I was sure it couldn't hurt me."

"What about your family?"

"They were very happy, and I felt that everybody was safe and that I could leave. Sierra was serene; she was as serene as the silt that gathers where the river widens. She was in a good place, but I wasn't, so I left. Nobody knew but Sierra. She wasn't happy to see me go, but she'd been with me for so long, and she knew she couldn't stop me. She was upset—more hurt really—but she wasn't going to try to get in my way. She wouldn't kiss me. She bit my finger, and my fingertips seemed so far away from me. I couldn't get Sierra's kiss from my fingertips to my lips; my hand just wouldn't do it."

"It was a bite."

"It was a nibble. I flew for twenty hours and ended up in Camp Rhino in the Andar District of Ghazni Province. I stayed there for four days and then went in country as an advisor with SEAL Team 3 in Paktia Province. I bought it on our thirty-ninth day out."

"You wanted to die, didn't you?"

"That's what I'm trying to make you understand. 'My path', as Conrad said, 'is to make you see.'"

"Who's Conrad?"

"Never mind."

"Are there any pertinent details?"

"Not really. It was pretty cut and dry; ambush, of course, and my payback. The kid stepped out from behind a boulder with a big, old Kalashnikov and squeezed off a round. I could have shot him first, but I was waiting for it. I watched him pull the trigger, saw the bullet explode from the barrel, and followed it all the way into my forehead. It took forever. I was thinking about my horse; thinking that I'd miss him."

"So, that's it, huh? Did they bury you at Rosecrans?"

"I haven't really been paying attention; figured you'd know that."

"Why do you think I'd know that? You've been wrong about me since you arrived."

"In what way?"

"You'll see. What else do you want to talk about?"

"Why, is our interview over? I mean, I've got a lot of questions. I want to know about the ancient ones—the Watchers, Confucius, and Lao Tsu. Who built the pyramids, the Mayan Temples, Stonehenge, the landing strips in Peru? I want to hear about Genesis—you know, the evidence."

"You've got time. The knowledge you seek will be revealed beyond your wildest dreams."

"That sounds kind of corny. What exactly is your story? What's your, uh, official position? Are you some kind of greeter or interviewer? Do you report to a higher authority, or is that you? When I was little, I didn't have any problems with an incomprehensible God; you were like Santa Claus, or the guy in the Michelangelo painting. I thought that Jesus was God's son, and that things didn't work out too well for him down on Earth, so he came to Heaven and answered the mail and listened to prayers. I thought JC was sort of God's secretary. Is that what you do?"

"I'm just here for you. I just wanted to get acquainted."

"Are my parents around here somewhere?"

"Your father is."

"Dad? Mom's not here? That doesn't sound good."

"It doesn't have to be bad. It's never too late."

"Wait a minute; who the heck are you? Are you a man, an angel, God, or something I don't know about?"

"You don't know anything. I am the un-man, the fallen angel."

"Oh, my God . . ."

"I just told you . . ."

"Oh, sweet Jesus, no, please, no, don't tell me. What did I do wrong?"

"You broke a Commandment, Monroe. You broke a real important Commandment—number six—it's a biggie. You broke it a lot."

"So, that's it, I'm in Hell? God sent me to Hell?"

"He doesn't send anyone to Hell; people sentence themselves to this place."

"Forever? Isn't there any way out?"

"There's always a way out, and I suspect you have an idea how to proceed. You named your child Anastasia."

"What's that got to do with anything?"

"The ancient meaning of your daughter's name is 'of resurrection'; it's Persian or maybe Russian. Anastasia Romanov was sainted."

"I didn't name her; Sierra named her, and what's her name got to do with me being here? Anastasia's name is just a coincidence."

"There are no coincidences."

"Says who?"

"Says me, and believe me, I ought to know."

"Well, okay, tell me what to do, tell me about Asia, give me some hope."

"There is always hope, but remember, false hope is a snare. There is always redemption and resurrection. Your life isn't over just because you died. You've always maintained a steadfast posture of unforgiveness; it's time to change that. It isn't too late, Monroe."

"This is exhausting. It's been a very long journey."

"No, it's been about average."

"But you said there is redemption, there is hope. God will give me a second chance, right? How long do I have to stay here? How long have I been here? How long have we been talking?"

"It's been awhile."

"It seems like forever."

"Be patient. Forever takes a while."

Edwards Brothers, Inc.
Thorofare, NJ USA
February 15, 2012